Praise about the Author

"Rikki Lee Travolta represents a by-gone era of rebellious icons. He is our decade's James Dean, Elvis, and Brando rolled into one."

– Chicago News Sun

"With Rikki Lee Travolta audiences know that they'll get their money's worth."

~ The Lowdown

"Rikki Lee Travolta... presents a powerful portrayal of the pain, perils, and promise of the maturing promise."

~ The Daily Bulletin

"Rikki Lee Travolta is a very versatile writer, moving easily from fiction and drama into journalism, and within journalism, from pop culture to hard core business themes and audiences."

~ Kirk Landers, Vice President and Editorial Director, James Informational Media, Inc.

"A Matinee Idol."

~ Suburban Chicago News

"A young sexy guy with a lot of talent."

~ G. Michaels, syndicated entertainment columnist

My Fractured Life

A NOVEL BY

rikki lee travolta

Copyright © 2002 by Rikki Lee Travolta

ISBN 0-7414-1267-5

Published by:

PUBLISHING.COM

519 West Lancaster Avenue
Haverford, PA 19041-1413
Info@buybooksontheweb.com
www.buybooksontheweb.com
Toll-free (877) BUY BOOK
Local Phone (610) 520-2500
Fax (610) 519-0261

Printed in the United States of America

Printed on Recycled Paper

Published October, 2002

Dedicated to the fans who make my career possible and all the fallen angels who have touched my life along the way.

A special thanks to my best friends Romeo and Gilligan, my number one fan Jeanna Marie Assman, and to my one and only forever – the divine Jessica Lauren.

Peace, Love, Trust

rikki lee travolta

In loving memory of

Angie Travolta &
Patricia Smith Landers

second star on the right

Jesse Newman was without a doubt the greatest actor I ever met. He also had the unattractive distinction of being the greatest talent that nobody had ever heard of.

I met Jesse when I was ten years old and we stayed friends for nearly twenty years. At the time I was a kid bouncing around the local theatre circuit thinking I was hot shit because I was playing lead characters in local plays, convinced that it was only a matter of time until I got discovered. That's the fallacy of youth – you think people are out there looking to give you a handout. The fact is, the world is not into giving handouts. People in power, whether it's Hollywood or in general business, are out for one thing – themselves. They have no interest in discovering or developing talent. What they want is to make money, and if you can help them do that then sure they'll use you. But, they're not going to go out looking for you – not when they have hundreds of people who fit the bill just as well lining up at their door everyday.

People are lazy. Why should a casting director spend money searching the globe for the perfect six foot blond guy when they can open their door and have their pick of 70 six foot blond guys? When it comes to film or television, the audience couldn't care less if it's *the* perfect six foot blond guy. You just tell them it's the perfect guy and they're going to believe you. Audiences are like lemmings – they'll follow the latest trend right over a cliff, even when that trend is as bad as N'Sync or New Kids on the Block.

Jesse and I met as kids in a Denver, Colorado production of *Oliver* – the musical based on the book *Oliver Twist*. I was the title character, the innocent orphan lost in the world. Jesse played the other lead child role, The Artful Dodger – a preteen conman with a heart of gold and a mischievous zeal for life, no matter what twists it throws his way. Even later in life Jesse always had that youthful glow. And his talent? He was nothing short of amazing.

He sang all right, nothing spectacular. But he could act like nobody else on this earth. And he acted when he sang. He didn't just break into song like so many "Forgive my acting but listen to my voice" singing actors. He made the song an extension of his character, with complete emotional displays that ran the register top to bottom. Sometimes I worried he was going to ruin his voice the way he threw himself into the emotion – screaming lyrics in distraught pain or whispering them in secret silence.

"Some people want to act, some people like to act, and some people have to act," he explained to me. "If I go out and do one performance the way it should be done and in the process ruin my voice, I'd rather do that than 10,000 performances faking it."

Jesse was a lush by the time he was a teenager – drunk or on painkillers for almost every performance and in most of his day to day life. I didn't know that until later, that's how damn good of an actor he was. You couldn't even tell he was loaded. He was a better actor drunk or high than most people could ever hope to be even with their full faculties.

I don't fault him for drinking, though. I basically had my life handed to me on a silver platter and have done more than my share of drinking and drugs. I do it because it doesn't much matter. I've never been too terribly talented. I was one of the 70 six foot tall blond guys outside the door waiting when some television producer decided to open his door instead of looking for a real talent.

Maybe I drink because I'm bored. Maybe I do drugs because I can get away with it. Maybe it's all out of guilt in an attempt to subconsciously sabotage my career to make way for the next guy who might fit the costume of fame.

Jesse had reasons to drink. He had the most amazing talent and rather than just rely on it he had studied with all the right teachers, joined all the right unions, networked with all the right people – but it didn't matter how good he was, he was never going to be allowed into the circle of fame because of who he was.

Jesse was an illegitimate child in a very famous family of actors. It's pretty easy for children in star families to get a break because of their family name: Angelina Jolie, Drew Barrymore, Joaquin Phoenix, Keifer Sutherland, Charlie Sheen,… the list goes on and on. But it's more than the name. There also has to be a "hey, throw my kid a bone" request of a favor from the family.

Jesse wasn't acknowledged by his missing-in-action father, much less that nonfather's family. That left Jesse with the choice of being a joke in the media by letting the tabloids exploit his illegitimate birth or by only working outside of the broad eye of the media, and thus never achieving the notoriety necessary for fame.

Newman, of course, was not Jesse's birth name. He changed his name when he was 15 in an attempt to hide his sordid lineage and achieve fame on his own. He never expected a handout from the family that didn't acknowledge him. But the family feared that if Jesse did achieve fame, even under an alias, some eager beaver reporter might still trace him back to his real name and bring shame on the family. So, in a world of favors and under the table handshakes, Jesse was forever blackballed. He worked under close to 20 aliases trying to win his golden ticket to Hollywood or Broadway. And every time he would get to that final stage – usually even get his contract signed and be ready to start work – the family would catch word of his latest rise to almost-power and arrange for him to be fired or bought out of his contract before he could hit the national airwaves.

You would drink too if you had to sit home to watch television because you couldn't get work, channel-surfing between three different prime time series that you had been signed to star in only to be mysteriously released. Or, if you had to watch actors without a fraction of your talent thank their families while accepting Emmy and Oscar awards for roles that could have been yours, had your own family not pulled strings to the opposite effect.

By the age of 21 Jesse had resigned himself to being an almost has-been, quit acting, and moved back to his childhood home. How about that? Not even a true has-been, only a could have almost been a has-been.

Before giving up on acting, his bread-and-butter was performing in regional shows, that's as big as the family would let him get. He was approached to take over leading roles in touring companies and even on Broadway; shows like *Rent, Jekyll & Hyde, Les Miz*. But those offers were because of his talent, not who he was. Once the producers got that call from the family politely asking for them to drop interest and at the same time offering a totally unconnected contribution to the company....well, let's just say Jesse never made it to Broadway.

When they revived *The King and I* on Broadway with Lou Diamond Phillips in the lead role, there was a huge national hunt for a replacement when Lou's contract was coming up. That was before Jesse quit the business. He was flown to New York to meet with the producers. It wasn't a cattle call where anyone but anyone could walk in off the street and audition, but at the same time it wasn't a private meeting. There were six other actors being considered for the role. The key was they wanted someone ethnic. There was one black guy, three Orientals, one Mexican, and Jesse.

Jesse always laughed telling the story. The casting director has them all lined up against the wall like they're in a police lineup or something. One of the producers is walking up and down the line like a General inspecting troops. As he passes each little actor-hopeful he voices the pros and cons of their ethnicity – that little voice you're supposed to keep inside your head, only somehow he's forgotten he isn't supposed to speak the thoughts out loud.

Or, more likely he feels he's too important to have to be politically correct and can say whatever the damn Hell he feels like.

"Hmmm, a little Mexican Chihuahua. That would be an interesting choice," he coos. Or, "Mmmmm I do love big black burly men." That's how it goes on down the line. A little critique on each man's looks.

When he gets to Jesse though, he stops dead in his tracks. Even Mr. Too Important to Not Say Things Out Loud knows that what he's thinking should not be said out loud. He more than undresses Jesse with his eyes, he licks him head to toe with his eyes. "I don't know what ethnicity you are, baby, but you are one damn beautiful man."

The call from the family came before Jesse could make his debut on Broadway as Lou's replacement. "Creative Differences" the producers cited when he was released.

Jesse was a realist. He only held on for a short time to the ideological notion that his eternal demotion to regional theatre was only temporary. After *The King and I* incident, he fired his agents and managers. It's not that they weren't doing their jobs – when they shopped his video reel of clips from his past performances, everyone wanted to hire Jesse Newman. But they couldn't fight the power of the Hollywood branch of the family. Jesse fired them because they couldn't do their jobs, because the family wouldn't let them. And anyone can book themselves for local theatre, so why dish out a commission for menial work that you can get yourself? One of the hardest days for Jesse was probably when he had to start listing his phone number in the phone book, admitting that he no longer needed an unlisted phone number. He didn't stay in the business much longer after that.

Jesse Newman took his fictitious surname from actor Paul Newman. Jesse actually couldn't stand Paul's acting. He thought Paul was a second-rate Marlon Brando or James Dean knock-off who had the good fortune of not getting fat or dying. But when Jesse met Paul in a chance encounter in a hotel elevator, the man

5

treated Jesse with sincerity. That was something Jesse respected. Jesse idolized his own family members in terms of their acting ability, but licked the wounds they inflicted in the way they treated him as a person. If he had to take another man's name, he wanted it to be that of someone he respected as a person. Acting ability had nothing to do with it. "Because," he explained, "acting ain't nothing but playing pretend. Being a good person is being real."

Jesse also happened to be the most reluctant sex symbol I could ever imagine. He made me look average. And I don't mean that egotistically. I know I have no talent as an "actor." I am cast because I fit the right shirt size, or more like because I look good without my shirt on. But Jesse, relegated to Nowheresville by "the family" still managed to have fan clubs from Dubuque, Iowa to Sweden. But he hated it.

I remember one time when Jesse was about 19 and had to work this mobile DJ gig to get by. That was the thing about Jesse, maybe his downfall in prospective. He never felt he was above anyone else. If he needed to pay the rent he'd scrub freak'n' toilets if he had to. People just labeled him as egotistical because they expected someone with his looks to be all full of himself. But anyone who actually knew him, knew he was the most humble man in the world. And even those of us who did know him and knew that about him, didn't know that he was such a tortured soul. He acted like it didn't bother him to be a nobody when he had the talent to be a somebody. How naive I was to not know how much that must have hurt him. He was the greatest talent I will ever know and he had to watch schlubs like me get rich off roles we had no business playing while he toiled away in mediocrity.

He had to embrace mediocrity. The worst thing that could happen to Jesse was if his name started appearing in the newspapers. Anything more than a mention in the local community gazette, and the family would find out and Jesse would have to move on to a new town. It was almost like Dr. David Bruce Banner on *The Incredible Hulk* TV show. He could never set down roots, because as soon as people found out who he was he'd have to leave. After awhile you run out of big cities to hide in; you start playing gigs in Northbrook, Iowa or Penski, Idaho.

Anyway, Jesse was working this God-awful DJ gig spinning music for graduation parties and wedding receptions. "I feel like a clown making balloon animals for the kids," he once reflected in one of those rare moments of honesty that Jesse rarely let show.

Jesse hated that damn mobile DJ thing for a number of reasons. There's the feeling like a clown thing, of course. But there was also the problem of being hit on. While he might have felt like a clown at those hokey hoe-downs, the patrons never saw Jesse as a wall ornament no matter how hard he tried to blend into the background. He couldn't get through a single event (wedding, graduation, retirement party, etc) without at least three or four of the attendees offering him their room keys.

I've spent my life as a slut. If I started my confession now I would still be going by the time I keeled over and died. So, I've always figured if I'm not going to get through the list of sins, I'm not going to get a chance to do the penance. And, if I don't even get to start the penance, I'm obviously not going to finish it, so if I'm going to burn in Hell anyway I may as well just keep on sinning rather than wasting my time in a confession that I'm not going to get to finish.

Jesse started out down a similar path as me. He was without a doubt the most attractive man I have ever seen. I mean straight as an arrow good looks. He was the only man who wasn't gay that I could honestly say was beautiful. Not effeminate, but beautiful.

Jesse was probably the most photogenic person I've ever met. It is a pure crime he was relegated to the stage. I say that like the stage is a punishment compared to film or television. That's like saying Heaven is a punishment compared to Purgatory or Hell. But a year in Heaven on stage doesn't pay as much as a few weeks in Purgatory or Hell. And, with all the unphotogenic, untalented people clogging up the lenses in Hollywood, they should have been beating the doors down for Jesse. But whoever said Hollywood types were smart?

Actors spend thousands of dollars securing the "right" photographer, getting the "right" wardrobe, having their hair and make-up done, having their teeth bleached, having their noses done – all to get the best picture possible. The headshot, the calling card of the actor: 8x10 black and white glossy with your name at the bottom and the phone number of the agent that the casting director will never call and who probably doesn't even remember you anyway. You could take a Polaroid snapshot of Jesse on a lazy afternoon with no preparation, no warning, and it would look more glamorous, more sexy, more million-dollar than any of those other actors could ever look no matter how much they paid, primped and prepared. It was his smile. His smile was electric; an invitation, a greeting, an assurance, and a promise all in one.

So, being a walking Adonis, Jesse had more than his share of women throw themselves at him. He couldn't check out of the grocery store without being hit on.

This, of course, started at an early age for Jesse. And he gave in to the advances. He thought they were genuine. He thought they wanted to be with him – Jesse, the person. He didn't realize they only wanted to be with Jesse, the body. He was looking for love and they were looking for a good time. Unlike me, Jesse didn't use girls, they used him.

At the age of 23 Jesse did a remarkable turnaround. I don't know if it was a moment of sobriety that made him realize he was being used, or if it was in one of those drunken stupors when you're so far gone that occasional brilliance can occur. Whatever the case, Jesse declared himself celibate until marriage – not throwaway, drunken fling marriage which actors are famous for, but true love marriage. He didn't go around shouting it from the mountaintops or preaching his virtue on others, but he refused to sleep with any girl from that point on until marriage. He wouldn't even kiss a girl passionately. "There's only one woman who I will kiss that way," he said. "My wife."

He wanted so desperately to be in love. It wasn't so much wanting to be in love as wanting to be loved. He had this fantasy that he'd one day be married with kids.

Sometimes we'd be sitting around shooting the breeze and I'd tell him we needed to go out and find some hot chicks to party with. "I want to find THE hot chick," he would always reply. His list of criteria was short: she had to love Jesse for Jesse.

Jesse was born to act, and when that was taken away from him, when he was forced to retire at an age when most actors first embark on their careers, he teetered on the brink of sanity. In a sea of confusion and lost hope, he drifted through a few pretend marriages and half-hearted attempts at a new career. Somehow he always managed to keep his feet on the ledge, off the edge. The pretend marriages came before his vow of celibacy, of course. That vow was probably the only thing that kept him alive to find "the one."

He was 27 when he found the girl he called "the one" – Andrea Kamp. He wasn't looking for someone to look good on his arm, but she did.

They met in a coffee shop. I was there when it happened. Jesse was explaining for the 10 millionth time what he was looking for. He'd gotten passionate in his quest. He was sure *the* hot chick was out there.

"Of course looks are important, but I am looking for something beneath the looks. I'm looking for someone who has a mind, who is my equal, who is my best friend."

From behind us in line came a shrill voice filled with feminist anger.

"You pompous men are all the same! All you care about is looks. You think you're so hot because you're all that, but maybe you should consider that there are girls out there who are more than just a hot babe in a thong."

We turned to see Andrea behind us, spitting venom.

"Miss, that would be an excellent argument if I had said that all that matters is looks," Jesse replied with that unfaltering calm of his. "But, what I actually said is that there are more important things than looks, such as a mind."

Andrea turned about seven shades of pink in embarrassment.

It was a year later, to the day, that Jesse proposed. He had known he loved her from the first moment they spoke, but he had been burned so many times that he had sworn to himself that he would wait at least a year before proposing. But, like I said, it was to the day that he proposed the next year.

When they first started dating, Andrea would do all the little things that Jesse needed to make him feel special. Because of Jesse's childhood and the cold shoulder he got from his family, he had pretty low self-esteem.

It's such an irony that people tagged Jesse with the label of having a big ego. I think it was more that they saw a good-looking guy – smart, talented, and from a famous family to boot – and they figured someone like that should have an ego. But the truth was that Jesse was just a scared little boy inside. I guess that's proof of what a great actor he was – he was my best friend and I didn't even have any idea.

But whether the outside world knew it or not, Jesse was a scared little boy inside a man's body. And he didn't just expect people to love him. He was always scared he wasn't worthy of being loved by a girl because his family had made him feel he wasn't worthy of being loved at all.

His mother had loved him. She lived for him. With her support he could take the doors of opportunity slamming in his face. But he lost her around the same time he gave up on acting for good. I guess that the events went hand in hand should come as no surprise.

I don't know if Jesse confessed all that to Andrea, although I doubt it. But she did the little things to make him feel he was loved.

For once in his life Jesse actually felt loved. And so, for once in his life, Jesse felt he was worthy of being loved. And so he proposed to Andrea; and she said yes. I was asked to be the best man, so I was in on some of the wedding plans, but not much. I mean, it's the bride's day, right?

The guest list was the start of their problems. Andrea would ask Jesse for the list of people he wanted to invite, Jesse would say he already gave it to her.

"I mean the people from your side," she'd ask again. Jesse didn't understand.

Andrea was asking a question without asking it. She'd drop the issue for a few days or weeks, and then come back to it. Always the same routine: she'd ask for his list, he'd say he gave it to her, she'd drop the subject.

"Why don't you ever talk about your family?" Andrea asked one day. It was a casual question.

"I do, honey. I told you about how me and my cousin used to work on the farm in the summers," Jesse said, listing off a series of conversations they'd had about his family.

"I showed you pictures of my mom," he added.

That spoke volumes. While she was alive his mother was his biggest fan and support system. When she died, the loss had hit him hard. The painful act of pulling out those pictures of his mother was a sign of just how much he wanted to share with his future wife.

"Not them," clarified Andrea of Jesse's reference to the only family he knew. "The other part of your family."

She was, of course, referring to the famous side of his family, the side that only acknowledged his existence enough to keep the rest of the world from knowing about it.

Jesse shrugged. "Not much to tell, I guess."

11

Who knows if there was awkward silence or casual conversation after that. That's as much of the story as Jesse ever passed on. The subject was dropped from active conversation for a time, but lurked beneath the delicate web of their relationship.

"You should write to them," Andrea urged a few weeks later, reopening the matter. "Or, you could call them," she offered. "I'm sure your agent could get their number."

Jesse didn't respond. What could he say?

Up until now Andrea had been the picture of decorum, bubbly and sweet. But now, a hint of that venom that had streaked their first conversation was in her voice. "Don't you want to know about them?"

The usually talkative Jesse shrugged again. He was the little boy inside, hiding from the monsters under the bed that Andrea was inviting to come out.

"They don't want to know about me. I'm not going to force myself into their lives."

"Jesus Christ, it'd be nice to think that I was important enough to you to want your family to be at our wedding!"

The venom in Andrea's voice was no longer just a hint. She threw down the invitations she was addressing and stormed out of the room.

It went on like that for a few months. More and more often Andrea would find ways to weave Jesse's family into the conversation, then prod him to open the doors of communication with them. She didn't understand that Jesse had long ago given up ramming his head against a door that would never open and that he wasn't the one who put the deadbolt on that door.

After a while Andrea stopped even trying to find nonchalant ways to bring the subject up.

"I contacted a private detective who can get their phone number for you," she volunteered.

Jesse gave up responding. He turned on the deaf ears. Of course they weren't really deaf ears, he heard every question. He just pretended not to. He was good at pretending not to hear, not to feel. He'd been doing it all his life. The precious family that Andrea was so adamant in pursuing had long ago wounded Jesse into hiding his feelings and pain.

One day Jesse came home and Andrea's things were gone. No note. Nothing. Just gone. He didn't want to know why she left, but he did. She didn't want to be married to Jesse; she wanted to be married to Jesse the member of a famous family. I don't know if she loved Jesse and then got caught up in the idea of fame later or if she never loved Jesse and was always in love with the idea of fame. It was probably a combination of both. Not that it matters much. Jesse had given himself one last chance to believe he was worth loving and it was shattered.

Early in their dating, Jesse and Andrea had a fight while he was drunk. The drinking didn't cause the fight, but Jesse figured that while alcohol wasn't necessarily the problem, it sure wasn't the solution. So he quit drinking. After Andrea left, Jesse fell off the wagon.

The difference between me and Jesse was that I'm an alcoholic and he was a lush. I need to drink. I can't go without the bitter firewater in my blood and can't stop until I've had too much. Jesse didn't have to drink, he chose to drink. If I were to stop I would go into detox and get the shakes and the sweats and all that fun stuff. Jesse could stop any time he wanted. After Andrea, he didn't want to stop. He got in the cab of liquid oblivion and left the meter running.

It wasn't only his abstinence from alcohol that Jesse threw to the wind after Andrea. He also tossed aside his whole notion of celibacy. Before he decided to save himself for marriage, Jesse was quite the ladies' man – but even though he eventually deduced the girls were using him, he was at least always selective about who he let do so. Not anymore. After Andrea, Jesse was a pig-slut. He didn't care what a girl looked like. What little self-esteem he'd had was shattered.

"We all have our role in life and I just have to accept mine," he said.

"I'm in my slut phase," he'd laugh. It never dawned on me that it was self-deprecating humor.

But for all the girls he bedded, he always used protection. It wasn't out of any sense of self-preservation. As a bastard child himself, he didn't want to be responsible for inflicting the life sentence of rejection he'd faced on anyone else.

The only thing that rivaled the number of girls rotating through Jesse's bedroom was the volume of alcohol he was swilling. Both were motivated by self-loathing. He drank from the moment he woke up in the morning until the moment his vision and mind were blurry enough to pass out.

Some alcoholics drink in pursuit of the right level of alcohol in their bloodstream that will allow them to function in oblivion. Jesse didn't drink to function in oblivion. He didn't want to function at all. If he thought it was possible, he would have drank himself to death. Instead, he drank himself to small individual deaths each night in hopes they would add up to one final bow.

"We all want immortality," he said. "Some people have kids so a piece of them can live forever. Me, I'm going to pickle my liver so it will last forever."

Eventually Jesse gave up on drinking himself to death. He died of a gun shot to the head. It was suicide, no ifs, ands, or buts about it. He'd been killing himself slowly for years with the bottle. He just decided to expedite the process with a ball of lead and a little gunpowder.

"Second star on the right and straight on till morning." That's what his suicide note read, a direct quote from *Peter Pan* – the boy who wouldn't grow up.

It wasn't a plea, that note. People who leave pleading notes usually swallow pills and call 911 themselves because they don't really want to die, they just want attention. Jesse's note was a prayer.

Jesse never got to be a child. He'd grown up as a child actor, supporting his ailing mother, her only support system. Jesse went from being six years old to being sixty. How fitting that he never looked older than a teenager, the exact years he never got to experience. I think that's what Jesse was hoping for in death, to experience the childhood he never was allowed to have.

I was the one who found Jesse, what used to be Jesse. Normal people find a body and they call 911. TV stars aren't normal people. We call our public relations firm, ask them what to do.

See, image is everything. A TV star saves a little girl from drowning and it's good press. An actor finds a dead body and it's not as appealing. In this age of sensationalism, a dead body alone isn't a good news story. It won't capture the ratings. Instead there have to be innuendoes that implicate the person who found the body, especially if that person is famous. Suddenly stories suggest that they were lovers or enemies who had once threatened each other, anything to make the headlines bite.

So TV stars don't call 911 when they find one of their friends dead. We call our publicist. Then we sit around and wait at the dead man's house until our publicist, agent, and attorney figure out if anyone can connect us to the body, who should place the anonymous call to the police, and how many states away we need to be before the anonymous call is made.

And we do our waiting in the house where we found our dead friend, where the body still lies in the bedroom, because we can't be sure if we've been seen entering and surely don't want to be seen leaving.

So while I sat there waiting, I read Jesse's diaries. Book upon book of words from his life. Confessions of the emotions he couldn't share with the outside world.

All those years I thought of him as my best friend, and I never had a clue what he was going through. He was always Good Time Jesse. It wasn't until I read his memoirs that I understood him. It wasn't until he was dead that I truly knew him.

15

hopewell

I live in LA, like every other actor. Although I don't know if I qualify as an actor anymore. I haven't worked in almost nine months. I haven't worked since being the one to find the figurative afterbirth of my best friend's suicide.

Even before that, it's not like I was one of those struggling actors who waits tables and spends all their money on classes trying to get their break – the ones that do little community theatre shows for free just to convince themselves they're really actors and not waiters. Those guys are out pounding the pavement every day trying to get their break. Not me. Not only have I not worked in nine months, I haven't looked for work in nine months.

I came to in a McDonalds bathroom. It's not waking up that I'm talking about. I wasn't asleep. What I'm talking about is that moment when you come out of the fog after partying for a night, or a few nights, or a week, or a month, or whatever. You're functioning, you've been functioning – carrying on conversations, having sex, or making your way into the McDonald's bathroom – you just aren't aware of it. Not until you come to.

As far as bathrooms go, it wasn't too bad. That, I knew, wasn't necessarily a good sign. Well-kept bathrooms usually mean you're out of the city. It's kind of a rule – the closer you are to civilization, the nastier the restrooms.

I realized I stank – not as an actor, but literally stank standing there in front of the sink in the McDonalds bathroom. You know that stale smell when you've been out clubbing? Dried sweat, second hand

16

smoke, your own smoke, spilled drinks on your pants, nonspilled drinks on your breath...that's the fragrance I was wearing. Maybe that's why I'd come in the bathroom in the first place, to wash off the stench. Who knew how long that faucet had been running?

Of course my fears that the cleanliness of the bathroom might translate into geographic location were fully justified. I found out from the little cutie at the counter that I was in Hopewell, California. The sheer fact that the girl behind the counter was cute was pretty much a dead giveaway I wasn't in the proverbial Kansas of Hollywood anymore. You won't find a single model wannabe working in a fast-food joint in LA. I don't know if it's that they don't want to work around grease or what. Maybe they just don't think it's a good place to get discovered. They all seem to work at the mall – in those clothes stores that are lined up one after another and all have different names, but carry the exact same clothing. Well they either do that, or porn. Or both.

For those not familiar with Hopewell, California, it's little more than an oasis on the 101 between Los Angeles and San Francisco. This I discovered upon stepping out of the McDonalds into an irritatingly bright sunlight. That's the funny thing about Southern California. We have more tanning beds per capita than anywhere else in the world. Even though it's sunny all the time, none of us actually see the sun. Well, except for the illegals from Mexico who stand around in the day laborers' camp all day hoping to pick up some work. We don't use movers in LA. You just rent a truck, drive up to the camp and you've got your pick of workers willing to work the whole day for 25 bucks – no coffee breaks, no dropping boxes, just hard work.

I didn't have my sunglasses with me so I had to squint to take in my lovely Hopewell surroundings. Just what I needed, more lines around my eyes. I'd been playing teenagers for the past 10 years. Now all of a sudden my hair was thinning. Wrinkles were starting to show. It was getting harder and harder to stay in shape. It wasn't so much a fear of aging that had me worried, as the fear of being left without a "type."

17

In Hollywood – well, Hell, in any type of acting, from porno to Broadway - you are a type. There are the leading men, the best friends, the girls next door, the balding fat guys, the balding skinny guys – there are no individuals, just types. If you can't get George Clooney, you get Kevin Costner – they're the same type: "middle aged, ruggedly handsome guy." If you can't get Jim Carrey, you get Adam Sandler: "wacky, over-the-top guy who does butt jokes." If you can't get Meryl Streep, you get Glenn Close: "amazingly talented actress born without the blessing of covergirl looks and too proud to go under the knife to fix it."

I fell under the "wrong side of the tracks rebellious youth" type. I got a lot of work doing '50s and '60s period stuff. Everyone's always trying to recreate the James Dean era. Not that I'm complaining – doing the James Dean knockoffs is what made me.

Of course at the moment, I was in bumblefuck Hopewell with no cash, no credit cards, and no clue how I'd gotten there. Not that it would have mattered much if I did have some form of money. Hopewell consists of a McDonalds, two gas stations, and a Taco Bell. No bus station, no train station, no car rental agencies, and no cab companies.

romeo now

A lot of people think once you have your own series you're in the money. I guess compared to real work that's true, but it's not like everyone assumes. I mean when you go from being an unknown to being on a series you're not magically a millionaire. When you're an unknown you'll sign your life away just for a guest shot on a series. So basically when you're signed to a new series, they lock you in to a long term skin-and-bones contract — just in case the series is a hit and you do become the next whoever. It's on your second series that you become rich – where you go from being Joe Schmo on a show to it being *The Joe Schmo Show*. After I hit it big on *Then Again*, I never got that second series.

When *Then Again* ended I didn't want to waste my time with another series. I thought I was going to be a Movie Star. Instead I became a Movie of the Week Star.

Oh sure, I had my shot at the silver screen – anyone with their fifteen minutes of fame gets a movie deal, but if the first one doesn't float you're demoted to straight to video work. You can't even buy your way back onto a series, so you do movies of the week.

My "money shot" was *Romeo Now*. When the studio pitched it to me it was "*Catcher in the Rye* for the '90s". I was told Tom Cruise wanted the part, but they thought he was too old. It had everything – drama, romance, drugs, killing. Screw *Speed*. Screw *Interview with a Vampire*. Those scripts were nothing. *Romeo Now* was THE vehicle to send me into super-stardom.

After I signed on, the script went into rewrites. Come to think of it, I don't know if I even saw a script in the beginning. I pretty much signed based on the pitch. Damn was it a great pitch. Sometimes I wonder if they were just making it up on the spot. Probably. It was too original to actually have made it past the studio script readers.

After the first couple of drafts, *Romeo Now* was looking better than ever. Screw "*Catcher in the Rye* for the '90s", this was "*Apocalypse Now* meets *Catcher in the Rye*". God that sounds good on paper, but when you think about it "*Apocalypse Now* meets *Catcher in the Rye*" means a bunch of stoned soldiers show up in New York and shoot down a kid who has flunked out of prep school. I mean it just doesn't even make sense, right? Well, *Romeo Now* didn't have stoned soldiers or a prep school dropout, but it may as well have.

By the time we got to shooting we'd been through three directors and more co-stars than I can remember. My original co-star was a box office diva; after a few more rewrites I was paired with a TV has-been. Eventually we ended up with an "unknown talent on the brink of stardom." I think she does dinner theatre now in Florida. Actually I'm just making that up. I have no idea what happened to her – she dropped further off the face of the earth than me. I'm truly surprised I didn't run into her in Hopewell, California. Anyway, the director we ended up with had more screws loose than your standard Hollywood player. Let's face it, none of us is really sane or we wouldn't be in this million-to-one shot business. But this guy really was missing the cheese on his crackers.

First of all, he was French. Now I have nothing against French people. Vive la France and all that. The problem was that he didn't speak English – not a word. Oh, I suspected he understood at least some. I mean, how can you not? The guy is around English speakers all day long. If he turns on the radio, it's in English. If he watches TV, it's in English. I'm not saying watching reruns of

Happy Days is going to make anyone bilingual, but you'd at least have some vague recognition of words. Not this guy. He prided himself on not knowing English.

Secondly, he had never directed a film before. His father had. Through his father he had gotten work as an assistant something or other on some French film that won some kind of award at one of those festivals that stars go to just to be seen. And in Hollywood, foreign guys are cool. More so, anyone associated with a previous success – even a French success – is considered a hot commodity. Hell, they'd probably give the costumer a production deal.

So two days into shooting, Jean Paul Frenchy-boy halts production because he suddenly sees this movie as a musical. A freak'n' musical! In come the songwriters, straight off of their string of smash hit toothpaste jingles. Suddenly I feel like Elvis in *Blue Hawaii* – breaking into nonsensical songs for no reason whatsoever.

Then either Frenchy came to his senses or someone at the studio saw the rushes because suddenly it was decided *Romeo Now* was not going to be a musical anymore. The problem with that, though, was that we were already done filming it. Try to imagine *Grease* without the songs or *Oklahoma* without the songs. It wouldn't make sense. The songs tell part of the story. It's like sung dialogue. You take that out without replacing it and suddenly there are big holes in the story.

Romeo Now was already way over budget by the time they decided to unmusicalize it. Nobody was willing to fork over another penny towards the film, much less a few more million to shoot scenes to fill in the holes where the songs were chopped out. I think the thing lasted in the theaters for about a day. C'est la fucking vie.

Of course I slept with my co-star. I was a big time TV guy just off a hit series, she was a nobody. I was her personal Hollywood welcome wagon. I followed the Hollywood tradition, the same way Elvis slept with all his co-stars. We could have done a song about it.

21

god of thunder

Sometimes I wonder about Alex Trebek – the host of *Jeopardy*, the trivia game show where you have to answer everything as a question. I mean he sounds so damn intelligent on that show since he has all the answers on his little note cards. He gets to tell all the losers in that smug little game show host voice of his that they're wrong.

"Oh! I'm sorry. You were close, but the square root of the hypotenuse of a right triangle is actually some fucking number nobody really cares about. Better luck next time."

But what I wonder about is if he retains any of that information he's reading. I mean, when he goes to parties is he the guy everyone gathers around – just to listen to his little witty trivia quips? Or maybe he retains so much of that crap that he can't help but be annoyingly intelligent. Like, he's the guy at parties nobody likes getting stuck talking to because he has all the fucking answers.

Then again, maybe he's just an actor reciting lines like everyone else in Hollywood. I can't remember a single one of my lines from productions I've been in. You learn the words, you say the words, you forget the words to make room for the next words you need to learn. Maybe he's like that. He comes home from the show each day with no clue what he's talked about. He's the guy who always finds an excuse not to go to parties because he knows he'll be embarrassed by the fact everyone will be asking him trivia questions and he can't even remember his own address.

Considering I live in Hollywood, at least when not stranded in Hopewell, and am enough of a once-was to still get into the parties of the still-are, it's rather telling I've never come across Alex in social passing. Just because I've fallen to B-list fame, doesn't mean I haven't rubbed elbows with the angels who have not yet burned their wings for the inevitable fall from grace.

I've met all the "greats" – no matter if what you consider "great" to be based on actual talent or fluke box office appeal. It's not that big of a deal, and really not that hard to do.

As odd as it may sound, I consciously choose not to hang out publicly with the A-list crowd. The key word is publicly. It has nothing to do with them as people, most are quite wonderfully sweet. The thing is, they cast big shadows.

If I am seen walking down the street with Nicholas Cage, I become defined as Nicholas Cage's friend. B-list actors, more often than not, could be A-list supporting players if it weren't for our ego's getting in the way. But just because you don't see Brad Pitt, Will Smith, or Julia Roberts skipping down the street with your B-list favorites doesn't mean we're not frequenting the same closed-door parties. Like I said, they're sweet people. It's us second tier players that enforce the discrimination because we don't want any shadows ruining our celebrity tan.

Yet in all those closed door parties where A-list, B-list, and even C-list social butterflies mingle away from the public eye, I have never run into Alex Trebek.

Early in my career when I was still doing theatre (as opposed to later in my career when I was demoted to theatre) there was this funny little groupie who'd show up to all my shows. I wasn't famous yet. I hadn't done any films yet. I hadn't done any television. I was just a local actor trying to get discovered. Yet here was this groupie.

He wasn't a "groupie" in a typical sense. It wasn't some teenage girl out for sex. It was a dumpy teenage kid who may or may not have been gay, but wasn't following me around hoping for sex. He just was obsessed with my career. He'd be at the stage door after my performances waiting for his hundredth autograph, and when I'd stop he'd always quote some line from a previous show I'd done. The thing is, I never recognized the lines. I'd have to ask him what the line was from.

Like I said, I learn the lines, I say the lines, I forget the lines to make room for the next ones.

One time Jesse and I were watching *Jeopardy* and holier than thou Alex was on some Roman or Greek subject. Maybe it was comic books. Who knows? I just remember the question he asked. Well, actually I guess in *Jeopardy* talk, it's the answer that Alex was reading. It's the question that the contestant has to provide.

"This flaxen haired deity of thunder ruled the Nordic skies with his magical war hammer," Alex read off his little card.

"Who's Thor!" I barked at the TV screen.

Jesse looked at me questioningly. Perhaps because I had never talked to the TV before, at least not during game shows. Or maybe I was just interfering with his drunken stupor.

Not many people know it, but before I became an *actor* and changed my name, my name was Thor. Honest. Jesse was actually one of the few people who did know it. Like I said, he was just confused as to why I was talking to the TV.

See, my father always wanted to be a writer. I mean he was a writer, he wrote magazine articles. Not fluffy consumer magazine articles like you see in the checkout stand – *People, Sports Illustrated*, or things like that. Not news magazine articles like you see in *Time* and *Newsweek*. He wrote for trade magazines. Those are magazines that aren't for sale to the general public – mainly because the general public wouldn't want to buy them. He wrote articles on such thrilling fare as "Efficient Paper Mulching Techniques", "Vitamin Supplements for your Dairy Cow", and the ever popular "The State of the Prosthetics and Orthotics Industry."

What he wanted to be was a fiction writer – one of those crafty wordsmiths who could make the pages come alive. He wanted to

24

be a novelist or playwright. But as much as he loved writing, he wasn't good at it. So, he wrote the kind of articles you don't have to be a good writer to write. He never stopped wishing he had that gift of flowery prose. He knew what he wrote was crap. He never read any of the magazines he wrote for. But boy did he love to read books. The library was his heaven.

He loved authors like S.E. Hinton and playwrights like Tennessee Williams. While he liked their stories, I think what he liked most about those authors was their use of unconventional names. Names like Brick, Ponyboy, Chance, Rusty James. I think he always resented, or at least regretted, that he had been born with such a plain moniker – Lloyd. Not as plain as John or Steve, but not far from it. "An insurance salesman's name" is what he called it – sometimes with a remorseful laugh, other times just with remorse. He would have loved a name like Cage, Truth, or Blaze. But such was not his fate.

When I was born, though, he was determined that I wouldn't suffer the same fate he did. I wouldn't live my life burdened by an insurance salesman's name. No, I would have a name worthy of a writer's son. He named me Thor. As I said, he wasn't a good writer.

My dad was what you'd call a functional alcoholic. He never missed a day of work in his life. But he also never missed a night of drinking. He wasn't an abusive drunk, or a sloppy drunk, or a rowdy drunk. He just liked to drink.

Hell, unless you knew better you wouldn't even know he'd been drinking. He could easily have been a character on *Cheers*. There they were every night drinking – Cliff, Norm, Frasier - but nobody ever got noticeably drunk. Except of course my father was too responsible to drink and drive, so he did his drinking at home instead of at a bar. Beer. Lots of beer.

I never really knew my mother. Apparently neither did my father. They'd gone out a couple times when she got pregnant. He was young – twenty-two or twenty-three I think. She was younger

– late teens I guess. I've always had a problem remembering ages and dates. I actually forgot Christmas one year. They start putting the decorations out in October so you get totally desensitized to it. Unless you look at a calendar, which I have an obvious tendency not to do, you'd never know Christmas had arrived.

My dad is pro-choice on the whole abortion thing because he believes it should be every person's individual right to decide about their own body. With that said, if he was a chick I don't think he would ever have an abortion personally.

It's not because of a religious thing.

"Let's face it, a few cells don't qualify something as a human," he'll say. "If that was the case, cutting off your fingernails would be murder."

My old man is just a parenting type, that's all. That's why he offered to take custody if my mother would have the baby. Have me, that is.

So, that's what they did. She served as the human incubator and carried me to term. He paid for the medical bills and did his best to keep her from doing any drinking or smoking or anything during the pregnancy. When she popped me out she signed all legal custody over to my father and he never heard from her again. And he named me Thor.

exactly the same,
except totally different

I wasn't the original choice to star in my series. My series, ha! First of all, nobody was supposed to be the star of the show. It was supposed to be an ensemble thing – a core group of characters — and different episodes would follow and highlight different characters. But when I caught on as a teen heart throb, the whole scenario changed.

Go with what works, right? If the 15 year old kids are screaming for me at shopping mall appearances and only acknowledging my co-stars enough to ask them to introduce me to them, well... *The Partridge Family* wasn't supposed to be about David Cassidy either, but that's how it turned out.

As I was saying, I wasn't even the original actor cast in my role. If you ever catch the pilot episode on cable rerun-land it's some other cat doing my character. I never knew his name, I mean I'm sure someone told me at some point and I'm sure it's in the credits of that pilot but I never really paid attention. Acting is a very egotistical genre. We care about ourselves. The outsiders we care about are the ones we think can help us. A nobody that a nobody like me replaced on a nowhere series didn't fall into that category when I signed on, and doesn't to this day.

The series was supposed to be a *21 Jump Street* rip off. Rip offs are the norm for the industry. When *The Cosby Show* caught on, one of the other networks came out with *The Flip Wilson Show*. Hell, maybe it was even my network. I honestly don't remember. Flip's show wasn't around long enough to make a dent in my memory other than that it appeared, disappeared, and ended up as the answer to a trivia question.

Usually the rip offs fail. Some high paid executives may argue that the reason that they do rip offs is because while most fail, some do catch on. I figure it's more a case of high paid executives deep down know they aren't worth their salaries and simply steal the ideas of other executives not because they expect them to work, but because it's what TV executives have always done. At least that way they look like they're doing their jobs.

ER was a rip off of *Chicago Hope* and it far outlasted it. I mean, they both premiered at the same time – opposite each other if I remember correctly. But, *ER* was developed after word of *Chicago Hope* leaked out. At least that's what I hear. It doesn't matter though, *Chicago Hope* was just a rip off of *Saint Elsewhere*.

Miami Vice was a rip off of MTV – flashy cars, hip clothes, and people with tans shooting guns with music in the background. "MTV Cops" was how Brandon Tartikoff pitched the series.

There was never any question my series was *a 21 Jump Street* rip off. The producers didn't deny it. They were just jumping on the bandwagon and trying to grab hold of a coattail to ride. So, that's how they cast it: young naive guy with a cute smile, young model-like black girl, young Asian guy, and young heavy set buddy for comic relief who could also be killed off if the series started losing ratings. And, of course, the overbearing but sexy police Captain running the show.

After they shot the pilot for *Then Again*, though, *21 Jump Street* brought in Richard Grieco who was a major smash with the teenybopper fans. You have to understand that a pilot isn't like a regular TV show. A regular show shoots weekly. A pilot shoots one episode and then everyone goes their separate ways while the producers try to sell it to the networks. If a network picks it up, then the weekly episodes start shooting. But months can pass in between the time the pilot is shot and when it is picked up – if it's picked up. Most pilots don't get picked up. Enough time passes between shooting the pilot, pitching it to the networks, and getting a deal signed that the show you're ripping off can introduce a new star – like Richard Grieco. Or like me.

The network picked up *Then Again*, but they made one demand. Make my character less Johnny Depp and more Richard Grieco. So out goes the old, and in comes the new – my big break.

Richard is a pale guy who dyes his hair black. There's an old rerun of Tony Danza's *Who's the Boss* that Richard was on. I think he played some distant relative of Tony's character. Anyway, Richard had his natural brown hair color in that episode. I don't know if it was his idea to go black, his agent's, or the *21 Jump Street* honchos, but it worked for him and I don't think he's ever gone back.

Anyway, that was his deal: pale guy with disproportionately dark hair. I have a dark complexion and bleached blond hair. I was the exactly same thing except totally different. Exactly what the producers wanted.

The funny thing is, I had only just bleached my hair before getting the audition. My agent was furious. When she submitted me, I had dark hair, almost blue black. She was convinced that's why I got the audition – I was a pretty boy like Richard, and had the same features, hair, eyes, etc. She was convinced that the producers were looking for a Grieco clone. And truth is, they were. I was the only one at the audition who didn't have the black hair thing going on. Maybe that's why I got the part. I stood out.

Casting is a weird game. I'll never claim to understand it because it's a game where the only rule seems to be that everyone pretends there aren't rules even though there are. But not only are those rules unspoken, not only do they change every minute of every day, but you are required to pretend that whatever the current rule is has always been the rule even though it wasn't and in 10 minutes it won't be again. Sometimes it's that you're the right shirt size; that's why you get the part. Sometimes it's that you're the wrong shirt size and "fat man in a little shirt" is funny; so that's why you get the part. Sometimes it's that you just happen to have a memorable name and it's the only one the casting director can remember at the end of the day. For whatever reason, whatever the rule was that day, I got the part.

21 Jump Street didn't replace Johnny Depp with Richard Grieco. He was actually just supposed to be a guest star for a few episodes and then get killed off, that's how Richard tells it. But he caught on with the fans so they nixed the plan to kill him off. Hell, he was bigger than Johnny.

After Richard hit it big with the fans, the plan was to keep him as their ace in the hole. Johnny was making rumblings about using an out clause in his contract to ditch the series and pursue a film career. I guess the fulltime film aspirations were out of guilt for having spawned the forgettable *Cry Baby* in his part-time film career.

Anyway, the way I heard it, the producers went to Johnny and straight up said, "Look, we're not going to be pissed if you jump or not, but we need to know what's up so we can plan for the future. Right now we can move Richard into your slot if you're leaving, phase you out."

But, Johnny reassured FOX that he was going to stay on with the show. So, rather than waste two big draws on one show, the network green-lighted a new series spin off for Richard. No sooner did Richard leave to start shooting *Booker*, his spin off, than Johnny exercised the escape clause in his contract.

Hey, I wasn't there. I don't know what story is true. But I've never heard Johnny dispute that story. I've never heard anyone from the cast say anything to dispute that story or even hint that a piece of it might be the slightest bit exaggerated. I've got no gripe with it being true, since the whole confusion of "Johnny in? Johnny out?" and then the eventual Johnny out is what made people switch over and watch my show. But I think if that story is true, then Johnny should have been a more upstanding guy – he didn't have to stay with the show, but he should have let them know he was leaving. Richard could have carried that show for a few seasons, but instead both the show and Richard disappeared.

Like I said, I'm not complaining. I live a good life because of that. Johnny Depp's abandoning ship is what made my career. Sure, my career is for shit right now, but I still have the money from when it was good.

Actually at one point there was talk of a project with me and Johnny together. It was a music thing. Wanting to capitalize on the whole Boy Band craze, one of those hot shot producers conceived of the ultimate boy band featuring real Hollywood heart throbs. "Pretty Boy" was what they were going to call the band. The fantasy lineup had Johnny playing guitar, Keanu Reeves on bass, John Stamos on drums, Jamie Fox on keyboards, and me up front singing. But it never happened, probably because it will always sound better as a fantasy lineup than it would have sounded if they actually got us together.

Recasting a TV show after the pilot is picked up isn't rare. Take the *A-Team* for instance. Ever see the pilot? As an insomniac with a satellite dish, I've seen the pilot a couple times. In the regular series Dirk Benedict plays the role of Face – the pretty boy who can talk anyone into anything. In the pilot it was some other guy, weird looking – had chiseled features that would have been attractive if they were aligned. But, instead it looked like someone had knocked everything just a little bit out of position.

With that guy not fitting the pretty boy image, and with tough guy but not quite actor Mr. T and used-to-be an almost-somebody George Peppard as the only names carrying the series, the studio probably told the creators to go bring in someone pretty with a little bit of a name. That meant either Dirk, who originally hit it big with *Battlestar Galactica*, or Ted McGinley.

Ted is the all time vote-getter in the replacement to save a series Hall of Fame. He was the "distant relative" brought in on *Happy Days* when Ronnie Howard left. Then, he was the replacement on *The Love Boat* when they kicked what's her name off for doing too much coke. Everyone knows actors use coke. It's practically part of the job requirement. But a director or producer can only look the other way so much. If they are trying to look the other way, desperately trying to

31

look the other way and still see you doing it, then it's time to pack your bags and make way for Ted McGinley.

After *The Love Boat*, Ted was the replacement for the villain in the television sequel of the feature film *Revenge of the Nerds*. I think the television sequel was *Revenge of the Nerds VII* or something. And with Dirk landing *The A-Team*, Ted then ended up as the replacement on *Married with Children*.

Some people may laugh at Ted. He's never had his own series. He's always the replacement guy. He's never the first choice. He's never moved on to movies. But I'll tell you what, I wouldn't mind being in Ted's shoes. He has been on more hit series than most actors have auditioned for. And that means he's got residuals coming out the ass. Residuals, the money you make from reruns of your show being aired on cable at 2 AM, are what it's all about.

The other night I saw the guy I replaced on TV. Maybe it was a few months ago, I don't know. I'm real bad with time. Sometimes things that happened yesterday seem like they were three years ago, other times I talk about things from months or years back like they just happened the other day. The relevance of an event is how my mind seems to categorize the importance of things, as opposed to the chronology of the events. Which, of course, is odd in the sense that meaningless trivia like who won the 1976-77 NBA Championship (the Portland Trail Blazers) seems to be far more important to me than when my father's birthday is (I don't know). For some reason senseless trivia just sticks in my head.

I can't say I don't recall the name of the guy who I replaced on the series because I never knew it in order to forget it. Oh, like I said, I'm sure I've been exposed to the name – it was probably mentioned on the set at some point and I know it's on the credits for the pilot. But I don't think it ever mattered enough for me to have actually known it. Sometimes I meet people face to face, am introduced to them, yet two seconds after shaking their hand I couldn't tell you their name. I figure I only have so much memory, so subconsciously I must only retain the things that matter. Hell, given the number of brain cells I've killed over the course of my short life, I really have to be conscious of the amount of memory I've got left upstairs.

The guy I replaced was on TV doing an ad for some hair loss product. He wasn't billed as a celebrity pitchman. He was an actor playing the role of a guy who's losing his hair. It was the first time I've seen his face on TV since my agent showed me the pilot to prepare me for my audition. Back then he was the handsome Johnny Depp rip off, now he's a balding middle aged actor struggling to make a buck – prostituting his hair loss for a chance to do a national commercial. He probably wouldn't be caught dead in the light of day without a toupee, given the frail ego of the actor. But given an actor's equally ego-driven need for exposure, for recognition, he tossed that piece aside without a thought for the opportunity to do a commercial.

I have to wonder if depression plays a part in the aging process. You catch snippets of fallen stars years after their heyday and compare them to snippets of stars whose reputation may have gotten a little tarnished but who never fell all the way from grace, and there's a real significant difference.

Granted, someone who now has to work for a living, I mean besides playing make believe, has less time to work out and less money for all the facial cream rituals. But aloe vera and a tanning bed only can account for so much in terms of that fall factor. Leif Garrett is bald and fat – won't go out in public without a hat or a bandanna on his head. He fell to the bottom, is currently playing in a garage band and only seen on *Where are they Now?* specials. David Cassidy was just as big as Leif, had just as big of a substance abuse problem, but he always managed to at least keep working. Like me, David may not still qualify as a star, but he still has the glow of a star.

graceland afterlife

When I die, I don't want to be cremated. I have nothing against it. If you want to be ashes, be ashes. I know some people have this phobia that if they destroy their earthly body, they won't make it into Heaven. More specifically I think it's a fear that they won't have a body in Heaven. They just can't get past that whole earthbound mentality of a soul having to have a vessel.

Me, I don't know shit about souls. I've been on every side of the religious spectrum. Technically you're whatever religion your mother was when you were born. I didn't really know my mother. She was kind of a mutt – one half American Indian, some Italian I'd guess from pictures, probably some Scandinavian blood in there somewhere. So whatever religion I am by technicality of coming from her womb, I'm not even aware.

My father was Catholic, but not too terribly devout. I mean, come on, he had a kid out of wedlock with a woman he hardly knew. And then he converted to Judaism when I was about four. He converted, I didn't.

My old man has this weird concept about a parent's role in a child's spiritual development. He thinks a child should be free to choose their own path. I'm fine with that, even though it suggests more of a flower-child open mind than anyone would suspect of my father. But his view is on the extreme side. Dad's feeling is that a parent is such a strong influence on a child that offering any religious guidance at all will prevent the child from exploring his own path. Thus, my father not only didn't offer any opinions on religion to me, he wouldn't answer any questions either.

34

I was free to go to any church, synagogue, Buddhist temple, Indian tee-pee, or shaved head airport sidewalk I wanted, but it was up to me to get there. He felt that it would teach me to appreciate the importance of religion if I had to sacrifice or struggle to get there. So basically I just didn't go.

During my teens I explored religion a bit. I went to church with Jesse a few times. His mother was pretty holy-roller about her Christianity.

At first I felt highly out of place at Jesse's church. It wasn't one of those big stained glass, chant-in-Latin places. It was a small community church. The minister, or priest, or reverend or whatever he was called was down to earth. He made his sermons really understandable compared to a lot of churches I've run across since. And the congregation was very warm and welcoming as well. I was uncomfortable because I didn't know the first damn thing about what you're supposed to do in church. I was far more familiar with Jesus Christ as an expression of swearing than as a religious icon.

They did this thing called "pass the peace." I guess a lot of churches do it. But, I'd never been to any church that I could recall. I mean, my grandparents tell me they took me when I was a tot, but I don't recall that. Passing the peace is this point in the whole sermon/ceremony dealio where you turn to all the people around you and you shake their hand and say "Peace be with you."

Jesse saved my ass that first time. He knew I didn't know shit about religion. He wasn't too religious himself; he went because his mom made him. She was pretty sickly, even then years before she'd surrender to cancer. She couldn't get out of the house much, but she always had the energy to go to church.

Jesse wasn't bringing me to church to convert me, he was bringing me because he got extra credit points in Sunday School for bringing a friend. He also knew that if I screwed up the most basic of rituals like passing the peace, his mother would probably recognize me for the heathen I was. If that happened, she surely would never allow me to come along again. Thus, Jesse would never get extra credit in

Sunday School and wouldn't be able to go on the sleepovers and outings like movies, basketball games, and concerts.

So on that first pass of the peace, Jesse turned to me and looked me dead in the eye. His stare said, more than words could, "do exactly what I do." At which point, he stuck out his hand to me and dramatically said, "Peace be with you." I got the drift, grabbed his hand firmly back and reciprocated. Alleluia – the sleepovers and basketball games were saved.

The thing is, I'm kind of lazy. I always have been. I will work my ass off if I know what I'm doing. I just don't like learning how to do it. So, the whole idea of learning how to do the religious thing was kind of daunting. I mean, it sounded like work. But the people were fun, I liked them – especially once we broke off from the adults and went to Sunday School. And, there were some mighty cute girls in our Sunday School class – right at that age where little bumps start to make Sunday School girls look a lot different than Sunday School boys.

I wanted the best of both worlds. I wanted to hang out with the Sunday School kids, with their bumps. But I didn't want to have to be the kid who didn't know anything. And I didn't want to put a whole lot of effort into getting to know what everyone else already knew. So I corrupted them. When it came to corruption, I was the expert and they were the ones who didn't know anything.

Because of my attendance, Jesse got to participate in the Summer Sleepover at the church. The teachers took a liking to me, pitying the poor lost soul so devoid of religious background. Since my parents weren't members of the congregation I couldn't be considered an official member of the Sunday School class. Thus, the teachers theorized, I couldn't be restricted from attending Summer Sleepover for lack of extra credit points. Only members of the class had to have extra credit points. So, I was permitted to attend on the pretense that the experience would be one more step towards saving my soul.

During the day we read some stuff out of the Bible and then the teachers talked about it to try to make it make sense to us. I was just staring at Amy Longheard's breasts. She caught me looking and didn't seem to mind. So I didn't stop. I'm pretty sure the teachers noticed. They kept glancing at me in this odd way, raising their voices as they read from the Bible. I guess the increased volume was to imply increased importance – particularly an increase in importance over Amy Longheard's breasts. I don't know. Her breasts looked pretty good to me.

At dinner, one of the teachers made it a point to come over and talk to me. Counselors I think they called themselves, although I'm not sure on that. I could just be associating them with counselors at the drug rehabs, since they conducted themselves in that same kind of overly friendly way. "Counselor," I've realized, is the term one uses when they want to sound like an authority but have no degree to hang on the wall to back it up. That's not to say a degree means you know anything. At least half the "educated" people I know don't know shit.

Counselor Jason was too nice to say anything about me staring at Amy's breasts all day, much less the feel she let me cop as we did the "mass of people exiting through one door" thing kids of all ages do when excused from a class. He didn't even say anything about the glances Amy and I were exchanging across the room as he talked to me. He just kept clearing his throat and talking a little louder, asking if I was learning much, if I was feeling my relationship with God grow, etc. I broke myself away from Amy's twinkling eyes and perky chest long enough to look Counselor Jason straight in the eye and tell him how much I was learning and how thankful I was to be there. The frankness had the desired effect, and put Counselor Jason at ease – allowing me to return to my food, and my eye candy.

I don't think the stereotyping Hollywood does could have painted the evening around the campfire any better. Hollywood is an amazing maze of hypocrisy. An agent shops a script and is told the subject has already been done, it's not original. So he, the agent, comes back with the writer's experimental piece – the one the agent told the writer was crap and would never sell because it's too different. Being an agent, though, he's not above switching his tune if that's what the studios want. Find a demand and fill it. Of course the studio head has never

37

seen anything like it and shells out a few hundred grand, maybe a mil to this unknown writer for the rights. Big stars sign on, everyone wanting to be a part of the only fresh script to hit the studio system in years.

With the big name talent and their even bigger money contracts on board, the studio masterminds start worrying about if such an unproven idea will work at the box office. Nobody wants to dish out $20 million to Julia Roberts and $30 million to Tom Cruise to have the film fail. So the studios bring in a few safe writers they know. "Don't change the idea," they say. "Just make it safer." So the new writers do a neat hack job, taking out the really brilliant parts and putting in some stock love scenes.

Suddenly, Cruise and Roberts aren't interested anymore. Cruise doesn't want to sit around waiting for a dozen rewrites of what was once a good script, and he backs out to go do a sequel of some mindless piece of crap that he at least knows from the start will be a mindless piece of crap. Roberts just doesn't want to be left at the altar and backs out to go do the first light comedy that she's offered.

Now the studios are in a panic. They've already invested huge money buying the rights to this brilliant, never-been-done idea, and even more money having it sanitized into something that hasn't been done but has elements of things that have worked in the past. In their panic, they realize the only way to attract another star to the project is to make it totally safe. So new rewrite "experts" are brought in, because obviously if Cruise and Roberts left, the previous sanitation officers didn't do a good enough job.

Soon, the studio has a bona-fide gem on their hands. *Home Alone II* meets *Beverly Hills Cop III*, they coo. Chris Rock is brought in since Eddie Murphy isn't available. Julia Roberts is back because the project has a new name, is now a romantic comedy, and nobody can tell it's the same project she left in order to go do a romantic comedy.

The film comes out and flops, of course. The critics criticize, saying it lacks any originality whatsoever. Meanwhile, back at the studio, an agent pitches a script to the studio head and he's told the idea's been done. So the agent pitches the writer's alternative script, the one the agent said he could never sell because it was too unique. The studio buys it in a snap, topping whatever sales record they previously set. Tom Cruise is signed to play the lead. And Julia Roberts, looking to change her image after yet another failed romantic comedy, signs on to co-star.

Maybe somewhere in Hollywood there's a starving writer who has a totally unique take on the campfire scene of a church sleepover. But that's why they're starving. The campfire scene at this sleepover was just as sticky-sweet wholesome and predictable as any Hollywood bean counter could want. Counselor Jason played his 12-string, acoustic guitar and we sang Kum By Yah, and all those other holy roller hits.

And don't forget the s'mores! Oh boy, we did the whole campfire drill. We melted marshmallows and put them on graham crackers with chunks of chocolate, and the result tasted like crap and got all over the place, making a mess.

Anyone who has ever had a s'more, or at least attempted to have one (since most of them wind up on the ground anyway) will say they're crap. They're a pain in the ass to make, and they don't taste good even if you don't drop them on the ground. Hell, dropping them on the ground is the best thing you can do. Then you have an excuse not to try to eat the nasty thing only to drop it in the crotch of your pants, where all staining foods tend to fall.

Yet, somehow s'mores are a staple of the campfire experience. You never see the campfire leaders, like Counselor Jason, actually eating the s'more. They simply guide the experience. That's because they already know it's crap. But just like they were forced to endure the Hell we call s'mores when they were kids, they feel it is their duty to inflict this curse on the next generation of what they hope will one day be 12-string acoustic guitar playing campfire sing-a-long leaders.

It's very much like fraternity hazing. You hate it when you go through it yourself, but you zealously inflict the same torture on others when it's your turn.

Once Counselor Jason got his feel-good songs out of the way, and chocolate and marshmallow was creating a dense cloud of smoke from where it had dropped in the bonfire, the counselors tucked us little teenaged campers in with a nice prayer. Then they were off to the sanctity of their all-amenity cabins, leaving us to become one with nature in our sleeping bags.

Once Jason and the Cosmonauts were gone, we set to making the sleepover a nonsleeping event. Well, at least I set out to make it that way. And I didn't have to do much arm-twisting to get my little religious friends to join me on the South side of the line between Heaven and Hell. No longer was I the kid who didn't know as much as they did about religion, now they were the kids who didn't know as much as I did about trouble.

My dad was a functional alcoholic, but his taste was for beer — a rather cumbersome commodity to smuggle to church. Jesse's mom was an all out lush. There were two establishments that could count on her weekly visits: the church where she prayed for salvation and the liquor store where she could buy it in a bottle.

So we had raided her liquor cabinet. Don't touch the Scotch was the rule. The old lady was a big Scotch drinker, everything else she didn't keep track of. So we grabbed two bottles from the back of the liquor cabinet that would never be missed – crème de menthe and Canadian whiskey. If ever there were two elements not to be mixed, it was those two. But what did we know? We were kids, still untrained in the laws of what would induce bliss — or what would have the opposite effect.

With the cosmonauts gone, Jesse and I unpacked our treasure. Rather than invoke peer pressure, we took the route of "drink it and they will follow." In flimsy Dixie cups, complete with jokes on the side, we concocted our potion. And, sure enough, the others were soon triggered to ask for a taste themselves. Much to my pleasure, Amy of the sprouting breasts was first in line.

I don't think Amy and I needed much, if any, booze in our blood to lower our inhibitions. We'd been eyeing each other all day.

40

Drinking a tad just gave us the excuse to act on those impulses. Soon we'd left Jesse to tend bar and we were cozied away in her sleeping bag.

Some women complain that men don't know what to do in bed, that they have to be trained. I was on automatic pilot. My fingers teased the firm flesh of her breasts. Beneath her shorts, I massaged her gently. The whole time our tongues intertwined, searching and exploring. The flickers of her tongue acted as my guide, telling me what she liked.

The sport of foreplay is much like basketball. There are those players who have the body for the game but not the mind, so they can be taught only the fundamental skills. There are also those players who have an uncanny knack for the game that can't be taught. Yes, their skills can be honed and improved, but they have a natural ability that can never be matched by the ungifted no matter how much time and study is invested.

Amy could well have been Catholic, given the familiar grace with which she took hold of my manhood – or boyhood at the time. We were hot and heavy, me ready to soil the pristine virginal confines of her sleeping bag, when some little whining do-gooder started a mule-like braying in my ear.

"Jesse's sick," he whimpered over and over. "Jesse's sick."

After about ten thousand and one choruses of the Jesse's Sick song, Amy and I broke from our mutual exploration. Her sleeping bag innards were smeared with the tale of more to come, but not yet fully soiled – much to my displeasure. But while a bona-fide porn star may be able to perform with dozens of witnesses, a spotlight, and a camera, I was a boy not yet able to come to manhood with the whining of the Jesse's Sick song in my ear.

Whiner Boy was right. Jesse was sick. He was giving the campers a puke-a-thon demonstration to end all demonstrations. Crème de menthe being an artificial green added a whole surreal element to the display.

It was like something Dr. Seuss would write. Instead of green eggs and ham, there were green s'mores from the campfire event, green mashed potatoes and chicken from dinner, green cola from throughout the day. However, I doubt Dr. Seuss would have prescribed the accompanying odor. Dr. Seuss was always quite witty and fun, and visually the regurgitated green food could have met that lofty goal. But the smell was rank, pungent, and had already inspired several of the softer stomachs in the bunch to join in painting the scenery with unnatural green bile.

Not that Jesse needed help. Jesse was doing a fine job of projectile painting all on his own. In addition to his own hands, face, and shirt he'd managed to cover the sleeping bags of several Sunday School companions, added to the natural beauty of many of the trees and bushes, and even extinguished the campfire. And, let me just say the splendorous odor of crème de menthe inspired vomit all on its own is nothing compared to the added touch of crème de menthe vomit burning over smoldering s'more remnants.

I did my best to keep Amy from the scene. It wasn't so much an act of protection – I mean, how harmful can green mashed potatoes be? It was a selfish act, I must admit. Should she draw too near the stench of Jesse's art, I feared that she too might fall victim to the contagious abdominal eruptions many were now suffering. And, should that occur, our little love fest would most surely go from postponed to canceled on account of bile.

Whiner Boy, the little red headed wuss that he was, wasn't content to have interrupted my exploration for the treasure of Amy Longheard. He wanted to go summon Jason and the Cosmonauts. I, of course, told him not to. Jesse was in danger of nothing except for a severe hangover the next day – and even then, if he puked enough there would be nothing left in his system to cause a hangover. He'd just have sore stomach muscles from dry heaving. All summoning the elders would do was put a definitive end to my entanglement with Amy, something that was becoming increasingly imminent.

Telling Whiner Boy not to go summon Counselor Jason and his campfire friends apparently didn't do the trick. Whiner took a long look at me, took a long look at the cabin up the hill, and took off for the cabin. He ran like he must have known I'd follow. If he'd known I was going to follow, he must have also realized I was going to catch him. I felt guilty tackling a frail kid like him.

Kids like that don't understand what it is to be a tattler, they don't know any better. They're scared of everyone because they're smaller than everyone – not just physically, but emotionally in terms of confidence. So, they try to please everyone. They try to please their peers by participating in the fun until it gets out of hand. Then they try to please the adults by telling on their friends when it does get out of hand. For all their effort, they end up pissing off everyone.

Nobody likes tattle-tales, especially not adults, who would much rather just let the kids work the shit out for themselves. But once they're advised of the situation, they're bound by the honor of adulthood to intervene.

I tried dragging Whiner Boy back to the vomit-stenched remnants of the campfire, telling him soothingly that it was all right. But he was dead-set on making a ruckus. I had no choice but to pummel him. By that point I wasn't feeling too guilty about it though. He was just getting plain obnoxious. Finally quiet, with the threat that I'd really kick his ass if he started up again, I set Whiner down to cry himself to sleep. Then I checked on Jesse.

"Jesse, you okay?" I asked, not doing too fine a job of hiding my repulsion at the odor surrounding him as I patted him on the back. Jesse nodded and grunted, which was good enough for me. I grabbed Amy's hand and led her back to what had become "our" sleeping bag.

I don't know what offended Jason and his Cosmonauts more, the stench of alcohol-laden vomit covering the campground and many of the campers, or the stench of sex wafting from the formerly virginal sleeping bag of one Amy Longheard. I guess it doesn't much matter which was more offensive, I don't expect they were too pleased with either development.

43

Needless to say I was never invited along to Jesse's Sunday School sleepovers again. But, then again he, Amy, and a few select other "superior" students were graduated early from their class. See, that's the beauty of post-adolescent Sunday School teachers. They still have that childish fear of getting caught; they're still afraid of copping the blame for anything. So, rather than talk to our parents about the incident and risk being blamed for poor supervision, they decided the wise thing would be to forget it ever happened and figure out a way to remove the bad apples from the bunch in a way that wouldn't cause suspicion. When I asked if I could join the Sunday School class permanently, I went from non-class member to graduating member in a record time of three minutes.

The reason I don't want to be cremated is that when I die, I want to be stuffed. Not only that, I want to be put on display as the main attraction of a museum chronicling my career. I may never be as big a star as Elvis. Hell, I know I'll never be as big a star as Elvis. There are probably Elvis impersonators who are bigger stars than me. But I'll be a bigger attraction in death than him. Graceland can kiss my ass.

I mean where else can you go to see a dead star on display? Nowhere. And believe me, I'm not naive enough to think my minor fame in life is going to bring in hordes of devotees alone. That's why we'll have things like roller coasters, kissing booths featuring look-a-likes, and a bar stocked with only the liquors I used to drink myself to death.

Graceland brings people in because of Elvis's fame. I've done the tour and it sucks. You see a few rooms in a house where he used to live, and if you pay extra for the garage tour you see a few cars he used to own but may not necessarily have driven. And if you pay a few more extra dollars you can see the airplane he owned. But people go again and again despite the rip off, because of the legacy of Elvis.

I'm in favor of the opposite approach. I don't expect a whole Hell of a lot of people to be weeping when I die. It's not my fame in life that will bring people to my museum, it will be the allure of the absurd. And that will give me fame in death far greater than I will achieve in life.

Dolly Parton tried to do a Graceland tribute to herself while still alive with Dolly World. And it stunk up the economy. Nobody cared. But, I'll tell you what. You put the saline packs from her breast implants on display after she's dead and they'll be people lined up to the county line waiting to get in. Death sells. Absurdity sells. Put them together and it's the stuff of legends.

I guess I come from a different perspective on death. I'm not scared to die like most people. I've known how I will die as long as I can remember.

Every night I have the same dream. Sometimes it's in the beginning of the sleep cycle, sometimes the middle, sometimes the end. It woke me up the first few years. Now, it's just part of what happens when I sleep.

I see my death. It's the same way, every time. I'm at an awards function. It's night. The limo pulls up. Reporters and fans line the sidewalk. I'm not star enough to get the red carpet treatment, but star enough to be there, and get the front door service. When I get out of the car the flash bulbs are almost dizzying.

I can't see myself; the whole vantage point of the dream is entirely how I would see it. But I feel myself smiling. I feel my arm raise and my hand wave. That's about when time starts to slow. That's about when there's this distorted crack in the night. A gunshot sounds a lot different when it's fired at you. It's almost like your name really is on the bullet. The gun is your false friend, it's warning you with a warning it knows will be too late.

I can see the fear on people's faces. I see people ducking. It's all a split second before the crack, the boom, the shot. But in slowed time it's an eternity.

I turn, trying to locate the source of the fear. I see powder and flame erupt over and over. Each time the yellow and orange slices in the dark give enough light to glimpse the gun barrel from which they escape. Then it's all black.

I'm not looking to die. But when you've had that kind of a dream every day of your life, you accept it's going to happen. If I live to be 90 years old and I haven't been shot in my tracks attending an awards show, I'm not going to run out and hire a hitman to gun me down just to fulfill my destiny. But I've come to expect how I'll die. So I accept I won't live forever.

I've fucked up a lot in my life. I'm the first to admit that. But, I won't die wondering "what if?" When you know you're going to die, when you accept you are going to die, you don't hesitate. You try things that maybe in hindsight weren't that smart, but then again at least you know that instead of wondering about it.

On the flip side, knowing how I'm going to die has given me a bit of Superman complex. I'm willing to try anything because I know as long as it's not getting out of a limo to go to an awards show, I'm going to survive it.

That's the thing about not fearing death, you really don't value life either.

the apple juice club

I never went through that cootie phase most kids go through. I've pretty much always been a pervert. I don't mean like a peeping through windows, "playing" with animals, or stalking little children kind of pervert. I just mean I've always had a very healthy sexual appetite – ever since I was a little kid. What "sexual" meant changed a little with time, but not much. It was a pretty fast evolution from innocent kissing to "more."

I had my first girlfriend when I was three. She was this little black girl named Melanie who lived upstairs from us. Dad was still pretty young, so it was early in his career. With the childcare bills there wasn't much left over so we were living in Harlem. That's right, a wiry little blond haired Italian guy with a receding hairline and his lanky blue-eyed kid living in Harlem. Well, obviously the race barrier was never an obstacle for me. Melanie was cute and available and that's what was important.

I used to go up to Melanie's apartment and play songs for her on this little plastic toy accordion my Grandmother sent me. I guess in actuality it was Melanie's parents' apartment. But, in my mind it was Melanie's. I mean, that's who I was going to see. Her parents were just there to open the door for me and give us cookies. We always had those little vanilla round things. Tasted like chalk. But hey, when you're three and they tell you it's a cookie, you eat it. Heck, if they tell you it's paste, you eat it.

That was my first foray into using music to woo the female species. When I was 15 I got a guitar and started writing songs. I am arguably the worst guitar player that ever lived. I took lessons.

47

I practiced diligently. I listened to all the right influences: Stevie Ray Vaughn, Jimmy Hendrix, Elmore James, Prince, Eddie Van Halen. However, somewhere between the stereo and my fingers, something got lost.

But it didn't matter if my chords were sloppy or that none of my songs featured the obligatory guitar solo since I couldn't play anything but sloppy chords. My goal wasn't to be a musician, it was to get girls. Girls dig guys with guitars. It's like their ears drown out all the missed notes and just focus on the dreamy image of telling their friends that they're dating a musician.

Ironically, I was always kind of a natural on the piano. I could sit down without ever having taken a lesson and recreate songs from the radio just playing by ear. But, there were two problems with that. First of all, we didn't have a piano of our own. Secondly, and more importantly, you never hear girls brag that they're dating the piano player.

I wrote about three songs, all of them sappy love songs. I actually wrote more than three, but they either didn't make sense, sounded virtually like the other ones I'd written, or just sucked. But three of the songs were acceptable. Nothing that was going to end up on the radio (although by today's standards, N'Sync has proven that record companies can force feed just about any old piece of crap to the tin eared public), but like I said, I wasn't aiming to be a great musician.

My three songs were what you might call my wooing songs. If the fact that I was a "guitar player" (and I use that term loosely) wasn't enough to get a girl in bed, I'd pull out one of my three standby songs and play it for her. That alone probably wouldn't do much, but when you throw in the fact that I'd tell each girl I'd written the song just for her – well, that was like my own all access pass to the amusement park of her body.

By the time I was ready to start grade school we'd moved from the hustle and bustle of Harlem to the nothingness of Castlerock, Colorado. My father had secured a transfer as a correspondent for *Feed & Supplements,* yet another trade magazine. This time he was writing articles aimed at the modern farming community.

Castlerock wasn't actually a city, nor was it even a town. It was officially referred to as a junction. It consisted of a general store straight out of *Little House on the Prairie* except that it had refrigeration and a gas pump, a three-room schoolhouse, a church, and a volunteer fire department. I'd wager the population was about thirty if you counted a couple of the sheep.

Of course I had a horrendous New York accent. You can't live in New York one day without picking up that distinct abrasive tonality. Considering I had learned to speak in New York and had never heard a person without a New York accent – well, you can only guess how thick mine was. There I was: four years old, living in the middle of sheep country, and sporting an accent that may as well have been from Mars. The poor schoolteachers had to work with me after school every day to get me talking like an actual human being.

The school itself was just as much a throwback to olden times as the general store was. Each classroom held two grades. First and second were paired off, third and fourth, and fifth and sixth. It was so far to the next town that busing wasn't budgeted for, which essentially meant that anything over a sixth grade education was optional. Kids going on to Junior High would have to be driven an hour each way by their parents up to Amity, the closest town big enough to have a middle school.

There wasn't a kindergarten in Castlerock, obviously. Hell, just to get a babysitter my father would have to drive the hour to Amity to pick up a high school kid and bring her back. Good thing my old man wasn't much of a ladies' man because those kind of babysitter constraints can really put a damper on one's social calendar.

I was one of those "bright" kids. Given my old man's love of reading and his not-so-secret desires that I become a writer, he taught me to read really early on. I was reading books, granted short books with big type, by the time I was two. Math came really easy for me too, but I wasn't a fan of it and since my father's plans for me were on the literary side of the spectrum he didn't push that envelope.

Being a little whiz-kid by normal academic standards, plus being stuck in a podunk educationally inferior town, I guess it made sense to just pop me into school at an early age. Kids normally start first grade at 6. I was two months shy of my 5th birthday when I started.

The trouble was I was kind of on the short side for my age. So, given that I was in class with kids one to two years older than me, it really made me stand out as a divot in the grand height scheme of the elementary school system. That's when I learned the Tom Cruise factor that height doesn't necessarily matter. If you're cute, you're cute. Tom Cruise and Mel Gibson may have to stand on their tiptoes to reach five-foot five, but girls dig them anyway.

It was during recess that initial year of school that I first discovered I had some type of – for lack of a better term – animal magnetism far beyond just being cute. Let's face it, no one will really argue with the fact that in terms of traditional beauty Keanu Reeves is pretty far from handsome. Yet, he has that magnetism that inexplicably draws girls to him.

I was sitting eating my lunch by the baseball diamond talking with a couple of friends. Although I don't remember their names or even their faces now, they were probably my best friends at the time – given that in those early grades you change "best friends" every few hours.

My lunch, of course, consisted of a cheese sandwich and a bag of celery sticks. It's what I had every day. There's kind of two reasons for that. See, first of all my father wasn't exactly what you'd call a gourmet. We weren't living off boxed macaroni and cheese or TV dinners – nothing that extreme. But, his repertoire was pretty basic: hamburgers, hotdogs, steak, pork chops – the kind of heart attack inspiring things one learns to cook growing up in the Midwest like he did.

The other factor was that I was a pretty damn picky eater. Maybe it was because I was exposed to so few things outside my father's base menu. Or, maybe I just genetically didn't have a taste for a lot of things. But, whatever the case, I was a picky eater. And, my father was of the opinion that if you can find one thing a picky eater will tolerate you stick with it. So, cheese sandwiches and celery sticks were it for me.

For the sake of not having to keep referring to my faceless, nameless friends as "my one friend" or "my other friend", I'll call them John, Paul, and Peter. Actually, that's far too biblical for my taste. In honor of my father's adoration for obscure names, I'll call them Raul, Giovanni, and Marcel.

We were sitting finishing our lunches – Raul, Giovanni, Marcel, and myself – and two of our classmates, girls, came to join us. We of course had to be cool – too cool for them in fact. We pretended like they weren't there; ignored their comments; focused intently on our spectacularly vital conversation regarding cartoons or *Dungeons & Dragons*, or whatever the Hell we thought was cool.

Then one of the girls leaned over and kissed me. My first lesson that playing hard to get works wonders.

I didn't react – neither pulling away in cootie disgust nor returning the attention at all. I just continued with my conversation.

Again she kissed me. Again I didn't react. More kisses followed, moving from the cheek to the lips. Soon her friends joined in.

Finally Raul, Giovanni, and Marcel pulled me from my seat and pushed me away while shielding me from my admirers.

"Run!" Marcel shouted. So I did, although not for the reason Marcel expected. I wasn't repulsed by the kisses. I liked them. I liked them a lot. I ran because I wanted to see if the girls would follow – and they did.

It was like something out of a bad cross-genre movie you might see at four in the morning: *Robin Hood on The Planet of the Amazon Women*. As I ran, the girls gave chase behind me. And as they ran, their Amazon tribe (remember, given my diminutive height most of the girls towered over me) increased in number. Soon it wasn't just a few first grade classmates pursuing me, it was girls from upper grades as well. In my mind I was the swashbuckling hero, a la Robin Hood, being pursued by the sex-crazed Amazon women.

One of the teachers, Mrs. Franchi, saw the hoopla. I doubt any grade school teacher, and particularly one in a backwards part of the world like Castlerock, would assume a school's worth of girls were chasing a pint-sized first grader around the playground in lustful desire. She probably assumed it was a "pick on the little guy" game or something. But, whatever it was that she assumed – she started blowing her recess whistle like a runaway freight train.

Hearing the whistle, I knew the game was near done, but not yet over. The miniature gears in my miniature mind started spinning. Did I want to go out the champion – having outrun all the girls? Or, did I want to go out the champion – having been caught by all the girls? The concept of winning is all in your perspective.

As the whistles became more shrill, less air between blows, I beelined for the cafeteria entrance. The entrance to the school was on the second floor, up the top of a set of rather steep steps. This was where the teacher on recess duty usually stood watch. The entrance to the cafeteria was on the ground floor, a little alcove indenting into the building. It was also customarily locked – the perfect place to allow myself to get trapped.

With all the determination of someone who actually hoped the doors would be open, I tried the lock. On the chance this might be the one day they'd been left open, I refrained from actually depressing the latch – instead just yanking fruitlessly on the handles. As I felt the crush of supple young bodies surround me, I turned to accept my fate, doing my best to suppress my delight.

It took the whistle blowing Mrs. Franchi and two reinforcements a good ten minutes to break through the crowd of goo-goo eyed girls to "save" me. I'd long given up any act of lack of enjoyment and was systematically embracing girl after girl. They found me in a lip clench with Susie Meade. I had my hand down the back of her pants – not that I knew what I was supposed to be doing with that hand, just that it was inappropriate, and thus needed to be done. That afternoon my father was called in for a meeting with the principal. It was firmly suggested we look at private school options for continuing my education.

I guess my old man had already been looking into some private schools, not for the same reason though. While the two classes to a room system was the best Castlerock could muster, it wasn't challenging enough for me. As a first grader I was already delving into the sixth grade reading material and due to my height and age, moving up in grades wasn't considered a viable solution. So Pop had lined up a private school, two hours away in Denver, for me to transfer to after Christmas break. My little Casanova routine just pushed up the transfer date.

Every morning my father would get up at the crack of dawn to drive me the two hours to Denver to attend Jensen Rosen School. Then he'd turn around and drive an hour back to Amity to go to work. At the end of the day he'd trek back up to Denver to fetch me before completing the final U-turn for home. He didn't mind the sacrifice of time and wear and tear on the car because he valued my education; too bad he never got to witness any of the classes. It was about the worst education money could buy.

Private schools don't have to adhere to the same standards as public schools when it comes to teacher certification. Some private schools use this as an advantage, hiring experts in art as art teachers instead of artistically challenged teachers who passed the appropriate classes. Other schools use this loophole as an advantage to hire the cheapest teachers possible, the ones who can't get hired anywhere else and accept low salaries just to have a job. That was Jensen Rosen's approach. And, with the teachers all knowing they were lucky to have their jobs, they didn't want to rock the boat and risk the unemployment line. No kid, no matter how illiterate, ever failed.

Private schools do little things to try to make themselves stand out from real schools. For instance, instead of calling a kid's main classroom a homeroom, they'll call it base room. I guess the philosophy is that if the parents are ever smart enough to figure out their kids aren't getting an education, the school can point to these other wondrous advantages that aren't available anywhere else.

One of the "advantages" that Jensen Rosen School offered was instead of having a milk break for kids, they had an apple juice break. Instead of little mini-cartons of milk, students got little cans of apple juice.

One day during our apple juice break two of my classmates, Colleen and Diane, approached me and my friends Josh and Kurt. We were considered the cool boys. I'm not sure why. I guess somebody had to be. It's not like we ran for election. "Hey vote for me for Cool Guy." We weren't necessarily the best athletes or the smartest kids or the biggest guys. But, for whatever reason, we were the cool guys.

Colleen and Diane invited us to join their apple juice club. Actually it was more that Diane asked us and Colleen stood by. That was their routine. Diane was a scrawny all arms and legs little pixie with a mop of stringy bowl-cut red hair – kind of like Peppermint Patty had stepped out of the *Peanuts* cartoon strip. Colleen was her sidekick. One day Colleen would probably blossom into a beauty, but at the time she was your typical mousy little girl with brown hair and big doe eyes.

None of us knew what an apple juice club was, but at six or seven years old you go just about anywhere you're invited because you feel special for having been invited. So us cool guys followed Diane and Colleen into the woods behind the school. They led us to a little clearing where there was a fallen tree to sit on. Proudly they displayed their collection of apple juice cans sitting in the center of the clearing, nested in a pile of moss. Well, I should say Diane proudly displayed the apple juice nest. Colleen stood by quietly, as was her role.

"We save our apple juice here and then when we have meetings of the apple juice club we all come out here and sit and drink apple juice," explained Diane.

Six and seven year olds will go just about anywhere they're invited; at the same time if they don't like it once they get there they have no concept of politically correct protocol for leaving. They just leave.

Josh, Kurt, and I exchanged the expression that is recognized worldwide as meaning "this is stupid." And, without a word, we turned and started heading back to school.

"But you're a part of our club, you can't leave!" pleaded Diane. We didn't care, we kept going.

"Please come back," she cried after us. It would have been almost funny to us, had we cared at all.

"You can have our apple juice," she offered. Still we kept going.

"Colleen will lift up her shirt!" she shouted. We stopped.

Turning back towards the clearing we saw Colleen and Diane engaged in a hushed argument. Obviously Colleen had not been privy to the decision that it would be she who would be showing off her prepubescent chest. Diane noticed us standing there watching and quickly made good on her promise, hoisting up Colleen's shirt. But just as quickly Colleen pulled it down.

With the floorshow over, us cool guys started back towards school again. "Colleen will pull down her pants!" offered Diane behind us. Again we stopped. Again we turned around.

Colleen stood in the middle of the clearing, bawling her eyes out. Diane had already pulled Colleen's pants down around her ankles.

I'm never going to understand rapist and molesters. There is absolutely nothing sexy about seeing something forbidden if the person doesn't want you to. Seeing Colleen crying like that made me sick. I turned and walked back to school while Josh and Kurt descended the hill back to the club. I was no longer one of the cool guys.

in bad taste

There are many reasons I've never settled down with a girl. For one thing I'm still relatively young. When you don't have a house-in-the-suburbs lifestyle you tend not to marry young, if at all. Or, if you do, you tend to do it many times.

There's also the fact that I've never really had a successful relationship. That isn't necessarily a precursor to a long-term marriage, kids, and house payments, but it usually helps.

But even if I had a girl who I cared about, and who actually cared about me in return, I still doubt I'd have managed to do the settling thing. It's not that I don't have at least a little seedling of hope inside me that I'm due for that kind of normalcy in my life. But, as a general rule, girls like to decorate. They want the house to be "their house." Ironically, making it their house has nothing to do with their taste and everything to do with following what shade of walnut Martha Stewart is pitching that week.

I have very distinct taste. I want my home to be my home just as much as most girls want their home to have the *Better Homes and Gardens* illusion of conservative perfection. Most men that I know who have definite opinions about decorating are gay. And their opinions pretty much match those of women – except the gay guys are better at it. My tastes are definite, but they don't have much to do with the aesthetic ideals of Martha Stewart, gay men, or women homemakers trying to emulate either one.

Rather than blow my wad from the series on a lavish mansion, I bought a little place in the Valley. I blew my wad on investments. Of course I know nothing about stocks, bonds, options or any of that crap.

But I know that I don't know anything about it. So I found a broker who does, and let him do the work.

Amazing concept – find a trained professional and let them do their job without interference. I have been able to maintain a healthy drug habit and get by on B-movies ever since because of that. John has much higher profile clientele than me, but I probably have one of the healthiest portfolios with the firm because I don't pretend to know a thing and don't try to give advice.

My place in the Valley, though, I decked out the way I wanted. Since I'm partially colorblind I've always been partial to black and white – the contrast of pure black on pure white. The dining room is one big checkerboard of black and white tile. Some people say it makes them a bit nauseous, but I dig it.

I'm not totally colorblind, just partially. Most men who are partially colorblind can't see red or green. I can see red and green. It's dark colors that I have a problem with. Light blue I can see, medium blue I can see, dark blue is black or gray. The same thing applies to any deep color. So, in addition to black and white, I've also always been partial to bright neon colors – fuchsia, hothouse yellow, burning sun orange, stuff like that. I like them because I can see them – vividly.

Off of my kitchen I have an enclosed patio. I think it's supposed to be a breakfast nook. At least that's what I took it as – give the impression that you're outside without being outside. So I played up the theme.

The entire nook is carpeted in Astroturf – going for that whole fake grass to match the fake outdoors motif. As for furnishings, it's all patio furniture – complete with the umbrella on the table.

In the dining room I have this grandiose table fit for a king. It's not some million-dollar antique or anything, but it's big and ornate and flanked by equally ornate chairs. At the head of the table is my chair, a replica of an electric chair. I got that from the set of *Diminished Capacity*, one of my many forgettable straight-to-video film adventures.

If it's not enough that I make guests try to have "normal" conversations with me while I sit in that chair, behind me I have a life sized anatomically correct statue of me posed as Michelangelo's David. You either look at me in the electric chair, or if you avert your eyes you look at a plaster image of me in my birthday suit. I love private jokes like that.

To be honest, I hate hoity toity cocktail parties. But I like to throw them from time to time just to watch the penguins and Beverly Hills princesses try to pretend they're not offended.

One of those Tour Celebrity Homes shows profiled my palace of bad taste one time. I've never quite understood the people who watch those shows – the "Hey let's look at all the nice things someone else can afford that we never will be able to as long as we live" mentality. It's the same mentality of guys who read car magazines – "Wow that's a nice looking engine. I bet it goes fast. Too bad I'll never know. Better put the magazine back on the rack and go take the station wagon home to the wife."

I figured I'd use the show for what it was – a publicity opportunity. There is no such thing as bad press as long as the audience remembers you.

Before the camera crew arrived, I had a mini bar put in my living room, which is adjacent to the dining room with the naked statue of me. My mini bar, however, wasn't a tiny little fridge stocked with little bottles of booze. My mini bar was a pint-sized replica of a real bar, complete with a midget bartender I hired for the occasion. I thought it was hilarious. Apparently so did John Q. Public - it was one of the highest rated episodes they ever had.

I've always had a thing for oddball themes. I had my garage outfitted to look like the Bat Cave from the old Adam West *Batman* television serial. That's where I keep my black '77 Corvette – which I've always considered far more of a Batmobile than the one in the TV show or the movies. I even have the Bat Poles to slide down from my bedroom on the second floor.

I also have my *Star Trek* room. I'm not what you'd call a Trekkie. I don't go to conventions or masturbate over pictures of the cast. But I thought it would be cool to have a replica of the bridge of the Enterprise in my house. The difference is that everything in my *Star Trek* room is functional. The big view screen that Captain Kirk uses to look at distant planets in the TV show is actually a television in my replica. The communications station that the big-breasted girl sat at on the show has a telephone in my room. And the command seat, of course, has remote controls for everything.

The way I got hooked on the theme idea is through pornos. My favorite pornos are the ones that are parodies of real movies – *The Sperminator, 0069 James Bondage, Pump Friction*. And I have a certain fetish for videotaping myself having sex. So I decided to combine the two favorites and began videotaping myself having theme sex.

For a long time Scott Baio, Brett Michaels, and I were regarded as the Hollywood welcome wagon for new starlets. If you were a budding young female star in your breakout film or on a new hit series, chances are you'd end up in one of our beds.

When Angelina became the newest flash-in-the-pan, Britney Spears rip-off, first-name-only, teen singing sensation she ended up on my welcome wagon. While they marketed her as a little vixen, she was actually a pretty sweet kid. She didn't know enough to say no, which is the downfall of most sweet kids in Hollywood.

One night we were pretty coked up, actually maybe it was afternoon. Anyway, we decided to reenact her *Dangerous Desires* video – except where the MTV video is suggestive, we went all out. At one point I'm fucking her doggy style while she is lip-syncing to the video camera. The whole thing is a riot.

My relationships with starlets never last too long. Either they continue on their paths to success and realize they can do better, or their comets burn out as fast as they appeared in the first place and they're yesterday's news – at which point I can do better.

I liked Angelina enough to be one of the few who can probably remember her fifteen minutes of fame, but there was no heartache when she moved on. Her manager detoxed her at his estate so it wouldn't make the papers and I got a teary-eyed, been jonesing for days call on my machine that "her people" didn't think she should see me anymore, that she'd miss me, always love me, yada yada yada.

It must have been six months later that I got served with a subpoena by an expressionless man in an off-the-rack suit. Angelina, or rather "her people," were suing me for our little video encounter.

Now, had Angelina asked nicely I would have been happy to give her a copy. Of course getting a copy wasn't the point, the point was to destroy all copies. And to be honest I probably would have handed it over if it meant that much to her. My theme sex tapes are something I make for me, not for the world to see.

This whole subpoena thing really pissed me off though. If she had really wanted the tape, I'm sure she knew she just had to ask. Her record sales had been falling and so had her position in the media. A half-dozen new teen hussies were vying for her title of queen vixen and she needed something to keep her in the papers. An amateur adult film can cause quite a scandal and, in turn, guarantee lots of attention in the news.

Most people don't realize that about 95% of celebrity scandals are leaked to the press by the celebrity themselves (through their "people" of course). That was the whole point, if you ask me.

Not that I minded being back in the papers again. It doesn't matter how notorious the story, being in the papers and on *Entertainment Tonight* automatically gets you on the guest list for all the important hob nob functions. People want the chance to rub elbows with you – perhaps to find out if the story is true, but more importantly because they know there will be photographers and reporters stalking you and by being at the same function, they might get mentioned too.

Angelina's people made one big mistake in not explaining to her that it was all an orchestrated media circus. They knew I'd fight them in court over keeping the tape – not that I gave a damn about the tape, but because by fighting it I would prolong my renewed appearance in the spotlight — which worked out to their advantage, too, since Angelina got to share that spotlight. But they never explained to Angelina that they didn't want the ordeal over. So it was without their blessing, I imagine, that Angelina called me and asked me if we could sit down and talk. I told her to come over.

The truth is I always really did care about Angelina, always will. I loved her just enough to know I'd never be good for her, and not enough to try to change. That's why I never tried to keep her. We were both young, but I'd seen a lot more and been scarred a lot more in my time in LA. She would get there too, but at the time she was innocent enough to actually feel love for me and believe in it. She didn't believe in it enough to sacrifice her career, her managers told her I wasn't good for her career and so that was that. But she did her fair share of silent dedications of her love songs to me in concert.

Angelina showed up dressed very professionally, like she was going to a business meeting. She had this shy aura about her as if she wasn't sure what was going on or what her exact role was, but that she wanted it to stop. It was sweet in a sad way.

She'd been clean off coke for a while. Eventually the same manager who cleaned her up would push her back on the stuff when she started to lose her edge, in hopes of pulling one or two more albums and tours out of the cash cow before it went out to pasture. But for the time being she was straight. She still smoked pot, did speed, and drank. But no coke.

I, on the other hand, was in my glory days of cocaine enjoyment. It was still new enough to be fun and not a need. I would never turn down a fellow nose powderer in need, but I will never give even the hint of a whiff to someone who is still on the wagon. Once they're off the wagon, I'll share. But I won't be the one to help them jump off.

So while I kept excusing myself to "freshen up," Angelina went through a good two and a half bottles of wine. You could argue that she was trying to imbibe liquid strength to ask for the tape and end the media frenzy, but Angelina was always a hard drinker. For such a petite little thing, she could really hold her own and had the appetite to match.

We tried to talk business, but it didn't work too well. I had feelings for her, she had real feelings for me. I was coked out of my gourd on some really great Bolivian shit. She was drunk enough to not care about the tape anymore and only care about the moment.

In that plane of coked mind meets drunk mind amidst pheromones galore, a different kind of logic sets in. We not only ended up fucking right there on the table, we not only videotaped it – at her suggestion this time — not only that, but throughout the whole thing she kept turning to the camera and screaming, "Fuck my lawyers! Fuck my lawyers! I want to be a video slut!"

In court her lawyers argued that I should turn over the original tape because Angelina had no idea she was being taped, or what the ramifications were for such action. They argued I had manipulated a young mind, barely over the age of consent. They didn't know about the second tape at that point. They did soon though. It kind of took the wind out of their sails to see their client screaming that she wants to be a video slut.

I'm not sure why her lawyers pushed it to that point anyway. We all knew the trial was winding down and we'd lost our edge in the media. Had they dropped the case, me and the tape would have disappeared as quickly as they'd brought us out of the woodwork in the first place. I certainly wasn't pushing for the case to go on. While you're getting the media attention it's fine, but once that's gone, court is a pain in the ass. Maybe Angelina's manager forgot to tell the lawyers it was all a sham too.

After watching the second tape, the judge was a bit pissed off that we'd opted to show it in open court rather than give it to him to view in his chambers. That was actually my suggestion – one of those private joke things. I like to make people feel uncomfortable like that.

While the judge was none too pleased that his courtroom had been defiled with such pornography, he had to rule in my favor. The evidence that Angelina was not only willing, but knowing, was pretty fucking clear.

For better or for worse, these stories never really go away. I mean, who doesn't own a copy of the Rob Lowe sex tape from the Democratic convention? And that was never released for sale, it was just traded among lawyers who would then in turn give it to clients they were trying to suck up to.

It wasn't long before the original Angelina tape started surfacing around town. Not the second one though, since that was never out of my possession. Makes you wonder if it was her lawyers or the judge who dubbed the copies of the first tape and started handing them out like party favors. If her manager had been smart he would have sucked all the publicity he could out of filing the lawsuit and then dropped it before the tape could be entered as evidence. Nobody ever said managers were smart. They're like unqualified agents, agents not necessarily being all that smart either.

It's always a pleasure listening to my voicemail and hearing the critiques of my friends on my pumping performance. Good reviews for the most part, although one did make an interesting suggestion that I could have been lip-syncing the background chorus of the song as I fucked her. I've never been one to do backup.

When the tape started appearing around town Angelina's less than brilliant, but always eager, manager showed up at my door. The tape was out there, and he could no longer control the media spin. Managers don't like to be out of control. So he proposed that we license the tape and distribute it ourselves. This from the same man who sued me to not distribute it when I had no plans to distribute it. Fucking asshole. The next time I saw him was in court for assault.

We need managers and agents to do the dirty work for us, to think of the angles because they have no morals and that – having no morals – is what it takes to stay on top. But as much as we need them, I still hate them. Most of the time they just disgust me, or maybe amuse me. But this guy just took the cake. I had no choice but to kick his ass.

my own private idaho

After high school I went east to New York and Jesse headed west for LA. Our respective destinations were ironic considering Jesse had the "legitimate" talent to make it on Broadway while I've always been more of the all image and no substance LA type.

LA is the home for people who don't feel at home anywhere else. Maybe that's why people in LA don't have hearts. Or maybe it's just a coincidence that people in LA don't have hearts.

The fact is you will never meet someone who is from LA. Oh, a Hell of a lot of people live in LA, in its posh suburbs, and in its urban slums. A million people a year migrate to LA. But, nobody is originally *from* LA. Everyone who lives there has moved there. That's not to say no babies are born in LA, but if they're smart they move the fuck away as soon as they can. Whether they stay or move away, nobody admits they're from LA originally – how uncouth would that be?

Of course I always felt at home in LA. That is to say, I've never felt at home anywhere and since LA by nature doesn't feel like home to anyone, it felt like I belonged.

It's funny, I've probably been in every state in the country – either doing bad theatrical tours or shooting bad straight-to-video flicks. But it was always a quick in and out. I rarely saw more than the inside of my hotel room, or someone else's hotel room, when I wasn't on stage or on the movie set. I couldn't tell you a damn thing about Dallas, Philadelphia, Seattle, Omaha, Toledo, Buffalo, Des Moines, or Phoenix. But according to hotel bills, I've stayed in all those places.

LA is a Nation, not a city but a whole fucking other world, of people obsessed with being as unreal as possible. Nobody uses the bathroom except to put powder in their nose. Everyone has a perfect tan and a perfect body. That's the illusion we are all supposed to present. There are no blemishes on our faces or our lives. Nobody is real.

Jesse didn't go to LA because he was an LA type like me, he went west because of his mother. She had moved to LA during our last few months of high school. She'd always been sickly, but her health had taken a significant turn just before graduation.

She'd destroyed her liver from a lifetime of drinking. A similar dedication to nicotine had left her at the mercy of lung cancer that had spread too far and was discovered too late. She knew she was beyond saving; she moved to LA so at least she could spend her last days in the sun.

Jesse had stayed with me and my father to finish out the school year. He invited me to come along to LA, return the favor, let me stay with him and his mom. Considering the circumstances, it didn't seem right though.

I don't know why I had my heart set on New York. Maybe it was because I'd never been there; I'd never been to the East Coast at all. I can't tell you what goes on in a headstrong teenager's mind, especially if it was my own.

For whatever reason, I packed my bags for NYC. I had it all planed. I had been saving all year. I figured I had a good six months worth of rent covered, which I also figured was more than enough time to land a Broadway show. Setting aside my misconceptions about the ease of making a living as an actor much less getting on Broadway, my thoughts on the cost of living in New York rank as one of history's greatest underestimations. I couldn't even afford one month of rent in the city, much less six. I was, for all intents and purposes, homeless.

So, I did what came naturally to get by: I dated. Now that might sound like prostitution to the uneducated ear, but it wasn't. I didn't take money for sex. What I did was take creature comforts for sex.

In other words, the question was no longer "Your place or mine?" The answer was always her place, because that way I could have a place to sleep for the night and a meal in the morning. And, if the flavor of the night was stupid enough to leave before me in the morning – "Let yourself out when you go." – I could usually pick up some petty cash she didn't even know she had by doing a little digging in pockets in the closet.

Of course I knew this kind of existence could only last for so long. I was living night to night, bed to bed.

In all honesty, I hated myself. I felt like a prostitute. It wasn't the fact that I was having sex with strangers that made me feel cheap like a whore. It was pretending to care about them so they'd let me spend the night that made me feel dirty. It was actually only a matter of days before I landed a tour and was able to leave the big city. But to this day I can't forget that ugly feeling inside, that self disgust at the idea that I was able to prostitute myself like that, violate my own morals, lie to someone and pretend to care. I was always a drinker, but that's about when it went from being a social abuse to a perpetual one.

I was cast to play Peter in the Broadway-bound production of a musical based on the play *The Diary of Anne Frank* – the real life story of three Jewish families living in hiding during World War II. Often before a show premiers on Broadway, the producers will either showcase it in a large metropolitan area like Chicago or Washington DC, or they'll put it on a limited tour. There are two motivations for this. On the one hand, it creates a publicity buzz about the production. Secondly, it allows the writers and director to work out the bugs in the show, get it running smoothly.

Anne Frank – The Musical is perhaps the most brilliant comedy I have ever read, much less ever been a part of. Audiences were rolling in the aisles. From the stunning seven part harmony opening number "I'm in an Attic," to the mid-show stunner "The

Halls are Alive with the Sound of Music," to the triumphant finale "We're Off to See Hitler" – complete with Anne and her family frolicking with merry Nazis – the show was a laugh riot.

If you don't recall the successful Broadway run of *Anne Frank – The Musical*, there is one good reason. It was without a doubt the funniest comedy ever, but unfortunately the writer-director hadn't intended it to be funny. He didn't see the dollar signs in front of his eyes when the show started to sell out; he was busy being angry at the ticket buying public for not being high-brow enough to understand the brilliance of the work. The director started making changes, trying to "fix" the show so people would understand his dramatic vision. But the more he changed, the funnier it got.

The producers knew they had a gold mine on their hands. They announced plans that we were going to cut the tour short and move the production to Broadway six months earlier than anticipated. I was going to be on Broadway. The show was a hit.

Producers see dollar signs; they could give a damn about artistic vision. But Theodore, the dual titled director and writer, held the reins. He held the rights. And if audiences weren't going to play nice and leave the theatre with tears of sorrow instead of tears of laughter, then he was going to take his ball and go home.

We were in Boise, Idaho, wrapping up the final leg of the tour before heading to Broadway, when Theodore pulled the plug. The producers tried to sue, but with the way our justice system works it's still tied up in the courts to this day. Instead of heading for Broadway, I found myself unemployed and broke in Boise – my own private Idaho.

foosball, foreplay, and fate

I wasn't born famous. Hell, I was probably never supposed to even become famous when it comes down to it. So naturally I had my share of "real" jobs before the fluke of fame occurred. I worked retail, construction, office, and everything in between, beside, and sideways. I think one of the reasons acting always appealed to me was because of my short attention span.

A job is really only interesting while you're learning it. Once you know what you're doing you may still be interested during that first few months of "I'm going to set the industry on fire" bravado. After that, the monotony sets in. Most people stay interested in their jobs because they're stupid. Because they're stupid, they take a long time to learn the job, thus it stays interesting. We're talking years. Hell, some never learn what they're being paid to do; they love their jobs forever.

My curse has always been being good. I pick things up really fast. So after a few weeks or maybe a month, I seem to manage to be able to do my workweek in a few days, and sit around bored the rest of the time. Jobs don't stay interesting that way. Although I'm smart enough to know that I'm really not that great an actor – probably the only thing I've ever done that I'm not a natural at. Could be part of the reason I stayed interested in performing for so long.

Aside from that, acting also fits my attention span perfectly. The whole nature of the business is to do a job – in this case playing a character in a film or on TV or something – for a short time and then move on to a new job, a different role. In the "real world," job hopping every couple of weeks or months, even on a yearly basis, is frowned upon. But that's what you're supposed to do as an actor – go from gig to gig, part to part. It fits me perfectly.

After getting to LA, my friend Jesse took a job bar tending at a male strip joint: The Stone Pony. My Broadway-or-Bust tour of *Anne*

Frank – The Musical had busted and left me in Boise. I was managing a copy store while hoping to latch on to a new show – somewhere, anywhere. I desperately needed to get out of Boise, for my own sanity.

You see, I've always lived for action, and Boise is not going to be showing up on anyone's top ten lists of happening places. My first night in town for the show, I asked one of the locals at the box office what there was to do around town for fun. I'm thinking bar, club – what's the hot spot? His response? "We play a lot of foosball."

Figuring this guy to be a yokel off the turnip truck, I gave him my best smile of appreciation and booked out of there before he could invite me out for a whalloping good game of foos. At the hotel, I spruced up and stopped by the lobby to ask the clerk where I should point my sails for fun. She wasn't a looker, but she wasn't ugly. Pleasant-looking enough to be a wannabe and know where the really attractive people hang out, even if she was never invited to attend.

"Gee, I don't know," was her reply. "The baseball team is on a road trip this week." That's double A, minor league baseball she was referring to. It was about then I started to get this nagging sense of dread that maybe foosball guy wasn't such a turnip. Maybe playing foosball and watching glorified softball really were the thrill rides around town. A stop at the gas station and the grocery store, where I got suggestions of watching the high school swim team practice and a second nomination for foosball, pretty much confirmed it.

Perhaps I'm thick headed or stubborn, or maybe I was just in denial. I don't know. But rather than follow the directions to the local foos hot spots the girl at the grocery store offered, I decided to cruise the main drags in town in search of something that looked like a night spot. It didn't take long; the town only has a few major roads.

Although the pickings looked pretty scarce, I did manage to find a strip club with a good assortment of motorcycles out front. Granted, not many were Harleys, but at least they weren't those little crotch rockets that pansy-boys drive. Imitation hogs were probably as bad as the bad boys in Boise got, I figured, and ventured in.

I'm not a strip club connoisseur. I don't have membership passes at clubs around the country. Like most celebrities, I have a few VIP cards for really famous places like Scores in New York, but of course I got those after getting famous. Before hitting Boise I'd been in a dozen or so joints. They vary from town to town, mostly based on what's legal.

Some places the girls are really skanky. Some places they're real dancers who take it a bit too seriously. Some places they're models. Sometimes it's fully nude, sometimes it's just topless. In some towns if they're nude the place can't sell booze. In some spots the girls do three songs in a row, the first clothed, the second in panties, the third nude. In San Francisco I got scared and left when the girl started shooting things across the room. In Chicago, at one club the strippers doubled as hookers in the back room until the place got busted.

In Boise, the girls dance in swimming suits up on a stage and "patrons" (as they are called on wall placards explaining the house rules) aren't allowed to get within 10 feet of the "performers." The girls never strip. And the bars don't sell alcohol.

Within three weeks of my arrival, I was the foosball champ of Boise.

When Jesse's mother died, he called and asked if I'd come stay with him for a while. It was all the excuse I needed to hang up my foosball title and pack up for California.

It was my second or third day in town when I accompanied Jesse to the Stone Pony to pick up his paycheck. Denise Hamilton, the owner, was in that afternoon. She came up to Jesse and me at the bar to give her condolences. To most people this would not seem an appropriate time for business talk, but maybe that's why most people are not successful in business – because it is thinking about what is appropriate and what is not that keeps them from succeeding.

Anyway, Mrs. Hamilton, as she is always referred to by customers and employees alike, started with the "you must be a friend of Jesse's" line of introduction. After our exchange of pleasantries, Mrs. Hamilton cut to the chase. "I don't suppose you'd be interested in a job here as well?" she inquired.

I admit I can drink with the best of them. And I have probably ingested about every known alcoholic concoction at some point or another. This point is most heavily substantiated by the fact that I do not remember such consumption, but rather a collage of disjointed hazy manufactured memories pieced together from the retelling of my drunken exploits by friends, associates, and total strangers. However, as I admitted to Mrs. Hamilton, I have no knowledge of how to mix drinks and probably never would as long as learning the skill involved being in close enough proximity to the necessary ingredients that I might digress from the role of student to the role of consumer. "Oh, I wasn't thinking of a bartending position," she replied. Thus was born my career as a male stripper.

My career as an "exotic dancer" – or oiled up meat sculpture – lasted a whopping three weeks. It wasn't that I wasn't good at it. Let's face it, the job requirements aren't much. Basically if they think you look good enough to hire you, then you have the minimum qualifications. The ladies in the audience aren't going to be judging if you studied with the Joffrey Ballet. Amusingly, that was the one critique I got after my first "show." Mrs. Hamilton told me to dance less and work the audience more. "Let them fondle you more" is exactly how she put it.

The money was great. I was pulling in several hundred on a bad night. I think my first night, before I learned the art of being fondled for dollars, I took home g-string deposits of $550. Some nights I cleared several thousand dollars.

The hours were great. I had my days free to go on auditions, work out, get drunk, screw some chick from the night before at the club. Actually it was because I was free to do all those things that I ended up quitting.

One of the nymphs I went home with was a lady by the name of Virginia something or other. She was a bit older than me, at least near 40 if not over. But she kept her body taut and tan and had the sultry sophistication that Mrs. Robinson let loose on poor little Dustin Hoffman. I was drunk, but I didn't need to be to have gone for her. She radiated sensuality, sexuality, and just enough danger to be intriguing without being scary. And she did not disappoint in bed. My God! To this day I still count her as the single most earth shattering sexual encounter of my life.

What made things even better then Virginia's worldly technique in bed was her unpretentious morning-after routine. With younger girls the routine is usually some expectation they have of thinking they've started some wedding-destined romance because they gave you a blowjob in the parking lot and you agreed to come over to their house for another one. With girls in their thirties, the routine is usually the opposite – "Thanks, that was nice, but I have to work early. Did I tip you enough at the club or am I expected to pay you now?"

With Virginia there was no pressure to stay or go, no assumptions or embarrassment. "I'm going to the health club, want to come?" she asked, after a more intimate morning workout. She belonged to one of those posh-posh Beverly Hills clubs – the places where it's more important to be seen there working out than to get any physical benefit from the workout. And in spite of the fact that nobody really used the equipment, it was one of the best-equipped gyms I'd ever been in. That alone was a sign of the priorities of the clientele. The biggest muscleheads I've ever seen work out at gyms that have nothing more than a few barbells and dumbbells, none of them light enough to be lifted by anyone other than a metahuman steroid addict.

At the gym Virginia introduced me to Angela. Angela – "never Angie" – was an agent with one of the big three agencies. One of the toughest things for an actor to do is land an agent, even a bad one. Getting in with an agent from one of the top agencies basically requires you to somehow hit it big on your own first. These are the agents who can literally make things happen with a phone call. "Hi Steve, it's Jack. Look, I know you want Harrison for that war picture. We're definitely considering it. I'd really like to sit down with Harrison and make a decision, but first I have to find a vehicle for this new ingénue we signed." Reading between the lines isn't hard to do, when agents even bother. Sometimes it's as simple as "I need you to do something. Find me a picture for a twenty-year-old girl I signed. (favor to be named later)"

But those big time agents don't take on just anyone. They handle stars. If you become a star on your own, or through the actual hard work of a lesser agent, then they'll swoop you up. Very rarely will they take on an unknown. And if they do, you can be sure that unknown won't be an unknown for long.

That afternoon I was in Angela's office. The next day I had my first guest starring role on a prime time series. I quit the Stone Pony that day. Big things were coming my way. Little did I realize Angela was doing me a one-time favor as a friend of Virginia's. She wasn't representing me full time. After that guest spot, it was another three months before I got another quality gig – a long distance phone company commercial. In the mean time, I took a job working the door for a nightclub. But that guest spot did attract enough attention to at least land me a non-big time, but not-awful, agent who got me the commercial and eventually got me the series.

Shortly after I got my series Jesse moved back to Denver where we'd met and grown up. He was never cut out for LA, I guess. While I was struggling and living in the spare bedroom of the house he'd inherited from his mother, it kept the place feeling enough like home to be bearable for him. But once I was prime time gold and doing the ever-popular shopping mall meet and greets, the loneliness got to him. He knew I'd never be small town again, and I had been the only small town reminder he had. With that gone, he headed back for the real small town suburb outside of Denver where he felt safe, in search of something to replace the memory of his mother.

a b. lynn michaels production

I met my friend Rick when I was 16 years old. I was visiting my Aunt in Chicago for the summer and stumbled into a community theatre production of *West Side Story*. I was a late addition to the cast. The guy who had originally been cast in my role got a better offer to be Emilo Estevez's body double for some movie that never ended up seeing the light of day.

By this time, I'd perfected the craft of being the fill-in guy. If you had an actor go down sick or drop a show, I was the cat who could step in with minimal prep time and fill the bill.

You see, there are guys who go in and audition and do a mediocre job, but you know that with a month or so of rehearsals they're going to improve dramatically. In my case, what you see is what you get. I give a pretty good first impression, but that's also what you get at the end. That's what makes me ideal for television.

In television you don't have a few months prep time. So television producers are smart to go with someone who can get the job done right now over a guy who will suck now but could have been good if you gave him months of rehearsal time and hand-holding.

Anyway, the producer of *West Side Story* organized this little bonding night thing with the cast where we all went out to dinner at some local pizza joint. I know the liquor laws vary from state to state; in Illinois, the law required the bar to be in a separate part of the facility from the restaurant.

I had showed up with two dates. I guess I had watched too much of *Happy Days* when I was a kid, and had seen that in all the episodes Fonize walks in with two or three dates. I figured that was cool. So, I tended to date chicks with low enough self esteem to allow me to have another date on the other arm.

I guess what was terribly odd about that whole scenario was that these chicks with such low esteem who would allow me to pull that kind of juvenile crap were some of the best looking girls I ever dated. It was as if their appearance was in direct opposite proportion to their sense of self worth.

So I'm there at this restaurant with my chicks of the week doing the bonding thing with the cast, and Rick mentions a certain thirst coming over him for some of the liquid nectar of the gods, more commonly known as beer. I'd learned long ago that despite being incredibly underage I could buy alcohol anywhere as long as I acted like I should be allowed to be buying it there, so I volunteered to venture forth with my noble comrade on the mission for pitchers of ale. Rick was already of age, he just wanted company on the trip.

Upon entering the adjoining bar, Rick and I found ourselves in an interesting predicament. On the television in the bar was the heavyweight title fight. In the other room were our friends awaiting a pitcher of beer. In our hands was the money of our friends. So, we ordered the pitcher for our friends. Then, we sat down at the bar and watched the fight, drinking from the pitcher that we had bought for our friends.

By the time the fight had ended, we had finished off a good half of the pitcher. We decided to head back to our friends and face the music for having looted half the booty. It was as we approached the table that Rick displayed the one true moment of brilliance in his life. Slowly he slid his hands to the bottom of the pitcher and I swear to God his hands started to shake in an involuntary way that only a truly scared man can achieve.

"Quick! Hold out your glasses!" he called out. People in confusion do what they're told. Rick immediately started pouring the contents of the half-pitcher of beer into the outreached glasses, long before anyone could notice it was a half and not a whole pitcher. "They gave us a leaky pitcher," he explained, wiping his hands as he poured for effect. He was so God damned convincing I didn't dare laugh out loud out of respect for the brilliance of the performance.

Community theatre is a funny entity. In concept, it's people from the community getting together to put on plays for the benefit of the community. It's a place where a husband and wife can spend time together being productive, building scenery instead of sitting together like stumps on the couch at home watching mindless prime time crap on TV. It's a place where a shy kid can break out of his shell. It's a place where a teen from a broken home can find a family instead of hanging out with the wrong crowd. It's a place where people who enjoy performing but don't have the time or inclination to pursue it for a living can still enjoy being on stage. That's in theory.

The truth is community theatre is the home of the people who desire nothing more than to be stars, but lack the talent. It's a petty world of back stabbing and gossiping. A bad review is always blamed on the theatre critic from the local paper not knowing anything about theatre or else they'd be working for a real paper – the kind that doesn't waste time reviewing community theatre productions. Or, the critic clearly must have a personal vendetta against whoever didn't receive what they felt was enough praise.

Granted, that's a generalization. There really are some people who perform in community theatre for fun. There really are some people who want to give back to the community. There really are people who don't break down and cry if they don't get a part in a little local production. But they are definitely in the minority.

I remember this one director, B. Lynn Michaels I met in LA. She epitomized everything wrong with community theatre. First of all, she thought she was a professional among amateurs because she was paid $50 dollars to direct a show once while the actors all volunteered their time. And to hold up what she perceived as the image of a professional, she would refuse to ever talk directly to her actors. If an actor had a question, they had to pass it on to Lynn through her assistant director. Reciprocally, if Lynn had a note for an actor, it had to be conveyed by the assistant.

She was also the only community theatre director I ever heard of who tried to employ the casting couch. That's how I actually met Lynn. I was starring in the series *Then Again* and the girl I was dating at the time introduced me to Lynn at a party. Lynn was in her late forties and wasn't the type who wore her excess weight well. But along with her false sense of power derived from earning $50 a show, she also carried a false sense of appearance.

I may not have been Harrison Ford, but I had star power enough to not have to introduce myself for people to know who I am or that I'm an actor. And my face was on every billboard across the country advertising the show. Somehow the difference between doing television and films – even bad films – and doing community theatre escaped Lynn.

In the middle of the party I felt an unfamiliar hand making itself very familiar with my ass. Lynn leaned her girth into me in what I think was an effort to be seductive, and whispered in cigarette tainted breath "If you and me happen, I'll let you play Sky in my production of *Guys and Dolls*." Her production of *Guys and Dolls*, mind you, was to be held at a local church.

Hmmmm? Star in a hit TV series or sleep with an older lady, who probably wasn't considered fresh produce even back in her prime, so I could have the honor of doing a church play. Sadly, our paths of logic put us on different sides of the fence in how we viewed the no-brainer aspects of that decision.

Rick is exactly ten years older than I am, and is a great father and awful husband in a marriage so doomed it will probably drag out forever. He is practically pathological in his need to tell tall tales and can switch gears from screwing hookers and doing blow to being the doting parent at PTA meetings by simply putting on his pants and wiping his nose.

When I met Rick doing *West Side Story* he still had ambition. By day, Rick worked as a journalist, and from time to time he'd do a community theatre show for fun. He went through the normal job shuffle over the years, covering the metro section for a local paper, drifting over to the advertising field, and finally moving to LA in a quest to land a job with *Variety*.

Rick never got the *Variety* gig, but by the time I'd landed my series, Rick had managed to merge his thespian hobby with his writing career and was the staff theatre critic for a harmless suburban LA newspaper. He wasn't in the same league as the *LA Times*, but he made a decent living. It was the kind of smaller paper that reviewed community theatre shows.

I told Rick about my run in with this rotund B. Lynn Michaels seductress. He apparently had experienced his run-ins with her as well. About a year back, before he had the theatre critic job and was penning articles about plumbing for *Plumbers World*, B. Lynn Michaels had familiarized her wandering hands with his ass as well. "The name B. Lynn Michaels is synonymous with outer Los Angeles suburban community theatre," she explained. "If you and I happen than I'll let you play lead in *Bus Stop*." This time not a church production, but a Park District production hosted at a local grade school. Even without a hit TV show to fall back on, Rick made the valiant decision to giggle off her offer.

The casting couch concept works when the person being propositioned is going to earn lots of money or achieve lots of fame as a result. The bargaining power just isn't there when the return on the sexual investment involves performing in front of cardboard scenery to the local blue haired retirement home crowd.

Later, as a theatre critic, Rick was assigned to review: "A B. Lynn Michaels Production of *A Streetcar Named Desire*, Directed by B. Lynn Michaels, Produced by B. Lynn Michaels, with original dialogue by B. Lynn Michaels." Rick said it was one of the three worst shows he'd ever seen. Not so coincidentally the other two worst shows were also B. Lynn Michaels productions: Shakespeare's *Hamlet* set in an Amish farm town and a retirement home production of *Annie*.

Apparently Lynn's *Streetcar* concept was to direct the Tennessee Williams' story of lust, alcoholism, and rape as a comedy. Not just a comedy, but in television sitcom format – complete with queen bee Stella styled after Florence Henderson on *The Brady Bunch*. The quintessential modern day Neanderthal character of Stanley, immortalized on film by Marlon Brando, in her show was modeled after Bob Saget of *America's Funniest Home Videos*.

It was that show that prompted Rick to eventually quit his job at the paper and open his own dinner theatre. I guess he felt inspired that with B. Lynn Michaels around, there was no chance he'd ever be the worst game in town. Being better than B. Lynn Michaels isn't saying much though. After one fledgling season, Rick had to convert the theatre into a strip club in order to stay afloat.

urinal etiquette

I have no memory for dates and make no effort to hide the fact. I used to have this arrangement with my cousin Rachel. She'd call and remind me of all the holidays and birthdays and crap in the family. All I had to do was remember her birthday, December 7th. She wouldn't remind me of her own birthday. But as long as I remembered it, she'd keep her end of the bargain and play social secretary the rest of the year.

I guess Rachel got tired of that little arrangement, though. So instead of reminding me of birthdays and holidays, she'd send a joint gift from both of us and call me later to tell me what we got people. Eventually though she got tired of that arrangement too. I figure I probably forgot her birthday somewhere in there and that's what ended the deal, but if that's the case she never mentioned it.

I tried writing dates in a calendar, but I lost the calendar. I mean I'm sure I have it somewhere, but I'm such a damn packrat it's probably buried under a mountain of scripts I wish I was a big enough name to have been a part of. Either that or under the pile of scripts I hope I'm never desperate enough to have to consider. As much as I don't want to do those awful projects, and haven't reached the point where I have to yet, the fact is, I haven't bothered to throw those scripts out. And I'm not saving them for their literary value. I'm a realist, and my stock has been on a rather consistent decline for some time.

After Rachel stopped signing my name to gifts, I sent out a form letter to everyone in my Rolodex. "I do not remember birthdays. I do not remember holidays. It is not on purpose, I just don't. If you're looking for the thought to count, I'm not your guy. If you're looking for a nice gift, call me and remind me one week before your special event and tell me what you want."

Of course, this was an open invitation to the guilt surfers. Guilt surfers are the ones who would rather draw out an argument than find a resolution, and in drawing it out they will always try to focus on how you hurt them. Guilt surfers aren't happy unless they're miserable. They can't just be quietly miserable, though, they have to be telling everyone how miserable they are.

My father is a world champion guilt surfer. I sometimes wonder if he converted to Judaism not because he believes in the religion so much as he already fit the stereotypical guilt obsessed old man profile. In every conversation I have ever had with my father, he has told me he is about to lose his job. Taxes are going to force the company to cut back and his is the most expendable job, he'll say one day. The new boss hates Jews and since he's the only Jewish man on the staff, he'll certainly be fired, he'll say the next day. Another day the reason will be that affirmative action requires more minorities be in the company, so since he's a white male he'll be let go.

Maybe it's a game for him, to see just how ludicrous a reason he can come up with and then convince himself it's true. Maybe he just knows it pushes my buttons to hear him constantly whine. He's been with the company for 15 years now.

My friend Rick takes me at face value, he always has ever since we met. So, when I told Rick – via form letter – that I don't remember birthdays and that he needed to remind me, he did. And as a result he always gets what he wants for his birthday – including a trip to see his favorite band the Zeroes in San Francisco.

We were both living in LA. I was on hiatus from *Then Again*, and Rick ran his own strip club so he made his own hours. San Francisco is about six hours away by car, less than an hour by commuter flight. We decided to make a road trip out of the event and drive.

The Zeroes never achieved any great level of fame. Their first album was on a major label, but sales sucked so they got dropped. Their second album was on an indie label. Without major label funding, sales sucked even more. So the indie dropped them too. The last I heard of them, the lead singer, Sammy Serious, mailed me a demo of what they hoped would be their third album and asked if I'd back the release. I think the demo is with my calendar somewhere under a pile of scripts.

Given the not quite respectable notoriety the Zeroes attained, the concert in San Francisco wasn't at any major stadium. It wasn't even at any of the clubs. It was simply at a bar any local band might have played at. But I like small venues.

Even when it comes to restaurants, I've always preferred the small venue, hole-in-the-wall joints. Take Chinese food, for example. Those mass-marketed, chain store places always suck. The food is so Americanized it may as well be Chinese McNuggets. Obviously I eventually outgrew my childhood picky eater phase of cheese sandwiches and celery sticks.

General rule: if the restaurant is designed to look like it's been taken out of a stereotyped picture of a Chinese temple, the food will suck (as if restaurants in China are really in temples). Parallel general rule: if the staff can speak English, the food will suck. Beyond common sense general rule: if the staff is Caucasian, Hispanic, or some other "maybe the patrons won't notice we're not Chinese" race, the food will suck.

Good Chinese food is found in hole-in-the-wall dives made by a little family that just got off the boat and can't afford to waste money on made-in-Mexico-to-look-like-it's-Chinese decorations. The mother and father work the kitchen and the son or daughter runs the counter with broken English. That is where you find good Chinese food.

The best Chinese I ever had was at Mt. Prospect Chop Suey in a suburb of Chicago. The food itself is good, probably second only to the Golden Dragon in Portland, Oregon. But what makes Mt. Prospect Chop Suey so great is the experience of going there.

This place is a slight variation on the typical hole-in-the-wall family duties. Instead of old man, old woman, and middle aged son or daughter, Mt. Prospect Chop Suey is owned and staffed by a middle-aged couple. Thus, the wife runs the kitchen and the husband runs the counter. She makes great food, but even if the food was awful, it would be worth the trip.

If I ever knew his name, I don't recall it. And I know I never knew her name. So, to keep from referring to him as "the guy" and her as "the wife," I'll call him Chop and her Suey.

Chop must have learned English from watching "How to Sell Anything to Anyone" infomercials. His spiel is pure Herb Tarlek from that old show *WKRP in Cincinnati* – the salesman in the plaid suits who was convinced he was Joe Suave but couldn't sell the last meal on earth to Dom DeLuise.

As soon as you walk in the shop, Chop will jump up from his bored slump on the counter and paste on a ridiculously plastic smile. You can't help but love his smile because even though it looks faker than *Baywatch* breasts, you know he is trying so hard to look friendly.

Ordering is done at the counter – one of those glass jobs filled to the brim with worthless novelty junk that doesn't have a chance of selling. It isn't Chinese novelty junk. It isn't made-in-Mexico to look Chinese novelty junk. It is just junk: kewpie dolls, trading cards for sports nobody has ever heard of, plastic daisy chain necklaces, rubber animals with only a vague resemblance to the actual wildlife, miniature cars of no particular make or model but reminiscent of boxy sedans a lower-middle-class grandmother would drive. It's like Chop ripped off the novelty rack from a truck stop in the middle of the Ozarks and put his loot on display.

There actually are tables and chairs in the place. Two tables I think – both far too small for anyone to comfortably balance the massive portions of food they serve there. Although the pizza parlor red and white checkered, plastic tablecloths aren't exactly bright and new, I don't think they got worn out from use there. They were probably were used when Chop bought them.

To be honest I think Chop wouldn't know what to do if someone actually sat down to eat at one of the tables. There isn't even a way for him to get past the oversized counter to serve anyone at the tables. He probably would have to go out the backdoor through the kitchen, walk around the building through the alley, and bring the food back in through the front door. In short, it is a take out joint in denial.

For every item ordered, Chop will hastily type away at a big button, basic function calculator. His fingers fly on the thing – in one way, similar to how Old World Chinese flipped and flicked the beads of an abacus, but in another way reminiscent of a child who doesn't know how to type, tapping randomly on a typewriter pretending he can. Take your pick – he is either a mathematical whiz doing advanced algorithms to calculate the fair market value of goods sold, or he is creating a diversion with his hands while he tries to figure out how much he can get away with charging the particular customer in front of him.

Either way, the price is never the same from visit to visit, even if what your order is exactly the same. But, for each item – not each total order, but each item – Chop will proudly turn the calculator around for me to see and say "Oh, there you go. Good deal. Right? I give you good deal. Super bargain." The emphasis is always on the wrong words, or the wrong syllable. But his enthusiasm says he is convinced he really is the selling whiz of the century.

Once Chop is done creating each individual super bargain on each entrée ordered, he'll play with the calculator some more to come up with the master bargain for the whole order. Of course this figure never matches the actual sum of the individual prices he's painstakingly calculated and joyfully shown. Maybe that's why with the final figure he'll only flash the calculator to the patron before hastily shutting it off and stashing it under the counter with the Ozark toys. Chop will then wait patiently for payment, oversized perma-grin on his face. Orders are never started before payment is in the cash register. That isn't a posted policy, it's just something I've noticed. Even when I have called an order in ahead of time, I end up waiting the same amount of time for my order as when I go in and order it. Until he has the money, Chop isn't going to do any chopping.

One time when I was in San Francisco I noticed that a lot of the Chinese restaurants had two different menus – one in English and one in Chinese. And the prices on the Chinese menu were always much lower than in the menu I could actually read. So, thinking myself the victim of some language scam, I decided to order off the Chinese side of the menu. I simply pointed at an item at random and said, "I want this." The waiter argued to the contrary.

"No, no, no. You not want that. You order from other menu," he said, then turned the menu around for me to the English side. Determined, I flipped the menu back around and pointed again to something in Chinese. I don't even know if it was the same thing I had pointed to before. "I want this," I said again.

We went back and forth like that for some time. Finally the waiter gave up and scratched down my order on his little pad of paper. Proud of myself, I sat back and waited for my dinner. When it arrived, it turned out to be crow's feet or something of similar consistency and flavor. We can chalk that ordering experience up in the whoops column.

After the Zeroes concert in San Fran, Rick informed me in a hushed whisper that he had to pee. I told him I'd wait at the table.

You can tell a lot about a man by the way he conducts himself in the bathroom, specifically his relationship with the urinal. A man who beelines to the far end of a row of urinals most undoubtedly suffers from an inferiority-in-the-pants complex. A man who chooses the first available urinal is the efficiency type. The center selector is typically your man of confidence. My friend Rick is in the unique category of being a non-urinal guy.

"I can't pee here," he insisted after the Zeroes show.

Well, San Francisco bathrooms can be intimidating in some neighborhoods. I remember one club where all the guys would go to the bathroom in pairs, and it wasn't for someone to talk to. I'm not saying all bathrooms there are like that. But if Rick didn't feel comfortable at this particular bar, it was no big deal. We'd hit another bar or something.

When we got in the car and I asked him where to next, he said home. Home? The night was young, we were on a road trip. Besides, didn't he have to pee?

"I can't go to the bathroom anywhere but in a house I know," he confessed. Looking back, I find it absolutely amazing that in all the years I'd known Rick I'd never noticed his odd foreign bathroom phobia until then. Yet, there we were with his problem on the table and the closest house he was familiar with was mine, six hours away.

Even with me speeding, the poor guy could probably taste his own urine by the time we rolled into my driveway – with him squirming the whole trip, crossing and uncrossing his legs. To this day there are fingernail scars in the leather of the door handle from where he was grabbing on so tight. It made me have to pee too just from feeling his anguish on the drive home – sympathy pee pain, I guess.

Me? I'm a pee anywhere guy. I don't need a urinal. I'll pee at the side of the road, I'll pee in the swimming pool, I'll pee standing up or sitting down. Peeing is peeing.

rounding third and going for home

My friend Jesse was never the same after his mother died. The
first few months, I stayed with him. He was troubled – who
wouldn't be? – but he hadn't "lost it." I guess as long as he had me
around, there was a sense of home, a sense of his past. The reality
of the situation – that such a major part of his life, of his past, was
gone – was tempered by the presence of a different part of his past.

When I hit it big with the series, things changed. I didn't just
move out and abandon Jesse. I would have stayed living there as
long as he needed me. That's what friends do. You can call me
egotistical. You can call me a pampered star. You can call me
irresponsible or an overgrown juvenile delinquent. But I have
never turned my back on a friend.

But even though I was still living with Jesse in his mother's
old house, I wasn't the same kid who'd grown up with him. When
we were kids, I was the pitcher on the Little League team and
Jesse was the catcher. I was a shitty pitcher, but I looked the part –
and I had that leadership thing that coaches look for. I had a gun
for an arm. The father of one of the kids on the team was a state
trooper or some kind of cop and he brought his radar gun to a
game – clocked my fastball at 98 miles an hour. That was when I
was 14. There are pros who don't have that kind of power. But
alas, I was a one trick pony.

I couldn't throw any kind of change up – no slider, no curve,
no knuckleball. Even worse, I could hardly control my fastball.
From the time I started pitching until I was banished from the
league, I put 17 kids in the hospital. I wasn't exactly banished, its

88

just that some of the other coaches in the league hinted that I would be "strongly encouraged" not to play any more or I myself might end up in the hospital.

Through it all, though, Jesse was my catcher. He was actually a worse catcher than I was a pitcher. Jesse didn't have an athletic bone in his body. His old man didn't acknowledge him at all, and his mother's on again-off again boyfriends were the type of absentee father figures who only showed interest in Jesse during baseball season. So, to have a relationship with even a poor substitute male role model, Jesse had to play ball.

At least I had my fastball going for me. Jesse didn't even have trick one to pull out of his sleeve. He wasn't a hitter. If he made it on base, he would inevitably get thrown out long before he made it home.

We were a package deal though. Jesse may have sucked as a catcher, but he kept my rebel-without-a-cause ass in line. Hell, he was so good at covering for me that he made my pitching fuck ups look like his catching fuck ups. That only made me look better, which in turn gave the coaches all the more reason to keep Jesse – because without him, I didn't play.

When I hit it big on the series, I was no longer in the same world as Jesse. I was no longer a reminder of the old days. On the contrary, with my new-found fame I was a glaring reminder of how drastically things had changed. I was also an example of the fame Jesse's real father would never allow him to have.

To recognize things had changed, that time had moved on, was to recognize that Jesse's mother was really gone. Jesse couldn't.

Quietly Jesse put the house up for sale, packed up his Blazer, and headed back to Denver.

That wasn't how Jesse changed. That was actually Jesse trying desperately not to change. If I couldn't hold the old reality for him in LA, maybe being in his hometown would bring back that reality. Of course it didn't. He was back in his hometown, but it wasn't the home he remembered, the one he'd preserved as a memory locked in time.

The move back "home" to Denver was supposed to make Jesse feel less alone in the world. Of course it had the decidedly opposite effect. Sure, Jesse was back in the town where he'd grown up, graduated high school, and lived all his life. But, with the exception of a few stragglers, his old friends had all grown up and moved away. Forever fades pretty fast in those years after high school.

I guess that's when he got a little goofy in the head.

quoth the raven "nevermore"

The movie *The Crow*, featuring Brandon Lee in his final screen performance, is incredibly masterful. It succeeds on so many different levels: as a supernatural thriller, as a science fiction literary adaptation, as a heart breaking drama, and as a high-energy action piece. Sadly, Brandon had died during the filming, killed on the set by an accident with one of the prop guns.

Ironically it may have been that tragedy that made the film great. Filming wasn't completed, and the producers had to rewrite the story, re-edit the concept, to make sense of what footage they had. The result was amazing. But subsequent efforts to repeat the magic in sequel films with other stars have failed miserably. The urgency of trying to piece together something whole from scraps and discards transcended the original film itself, and without that real life urgency motivating the producers of the sequels, there was no life's breath to their work.

In the first *Crow* sequel, the film lacked a story of any consequence. But at least the actor looked the role – handsome and hallowed. He couldn't act, but he looked the part. The next sequel didn't even make it into the theatres. Like the first sequel, it was made without the benefit of a story line. Unlike its predecessor though, its lead actor – 'The Crow' himself – did not look the part. He couldn't act either, as if that mattered. Trying to sit through that movie was painful. The actor looked like Herman Munster from the *Munsters* television show. Was it the producer, the director, or the screenwriter who decided to cast a mongoloid? Were they trying to appeal to the Special Olympics audience?

As bad as the offshoots have been, I actually hope they don't close down the *Crow* franchise. Before I stopped returning my agent's calls, I was campaigning for him to pitch a new story line to the producers – for me, of course.

The basic premise of the original and its subsequent rip-offs is simple: man and his loved ones are murdered, a mythical crow carries the man's soul back to earth and brings his body back to life to seek revenge on the murderers. And when the man comes back to life, he paints his face in a symbolic reflection of the crow. In the original film, Brandon's character paints his face with makeup he had used in life as a rock star ala Kiss. In the first sequel the Brandon-replacement decorates his face with the finger-paint his murdered son had used in play.

With each sequel, the producers move the story further and further into the future. My concept is a prequel – a drastic prequel. I took the concept and put it in the old west, making the man who would be *The Crow* a Native American. Many Indian tribes believed in spirit guides, Gods in the shape of animals. When his village is murdered by white cavalry, one young warrior is brought back by his spirit guide – the crow. His face is painted in war paint as he seeks vengeance. I call it *Spirit Warrior*.

My agent actually does like the story line, really thought we might be able to sell it. But he's not sure they'll take me along with the package. Apparently my star, in my agent's opinion, is not as bright as a mongoloid's. I might just be a little too much of a has-been and not enough of a could-be to get the nod to star.

My friend Jesse called me up one night shortly after he'd moved back to Denver. The Sci-Fi Channel or one of those entertainment shows had run a biography on Brandon Lee. It included an interview he'd done on the set of *The Crow* just days before he'd died.

Jesse was freak'n' lit up over this interview, like he had just witnessed Christ's resurrection or something. He had taped it and keep rewinding and playing it over and over for me on the phone.

Over and over, Brandon talking about how cool his character is – the ultimate loner, walking around quoting Edgar Allen Poe all the time.

Jesse was an outcast, a man trapped in a memory of yesterday, surrounded by a today that had passed him by. He was alone, a loner by default if not by choice. In some goofy way that makes sense to outcasts and manic-depressives, Jesse felt the way to deal with his loneliness was to idolize the fallen icon of Brandon Lee, *The Crow*.

The kid who had never read poetry in his life, whose English Lit aspirations had always been remedial at best, was now memorizing entire books of Poe. He committed to memory and freely quoted the works of the sad poet with the fervor of a Born Again memorizing and regurgitating passages from the Bible.

Funny how we have a tendency to achieve the opposite of our intentions sometimes. Jesse embarked on his journey of gothic dress and sorrowful quotations as an embrace of the lone wolf persona he had fallen into. But somehow my young brooding friend was now even more irresistible to the ladies than ever. The more he shunned attention, the more desirable he became.

It's easy to see all that when it's not happening to you, even easier to recognize it in hindsight. But Jesse wasn't embarking on this little externalization of his inner mental breakdown in an effort to get girls. He wanted to not be alone so badly that he had created this character out of self-pity. He ended up marrying the first girl to give him the time of day.

Patty was her name. She had two kids – Christian and Taylor. For Jesse it was the ready-made family. He moved from being alone to having a family, kids and all.

Patty was the epitome of trailer trash. I only ever had a chance to really have a conversation with her once, so I can't comment on her personality or anything like that. But she was literally trailer trash. Patty literally lived in a two-trailer conglomeration with her parents; her two kids from different fathers; her pregnant sister and her boyfriend; her half-brother, his girlfriend, and his son from a previous girlfriend; and her half-sister, whose daughter lived with the father's mother but visited from time to time.

As immersed in the trailer park as her life may have been, Patty did disprove the stereotype that all such colorful characters are country bumpkins. Patty was a law student, pretty near the top of her class. Just getting through law school would be a chore for most; Hell, let's face it, getting into law school is beyond the capabilities of many a well-educated socialite. Not only was Patty skating through the drudgeries of graduate school, she'd managed to convince Uncle Sam that having two children by different absentee fathers was reason enough to pick up the tab for her schooling. Uncle Sam was actually so impressed with little Miss Patty's ability to produce illegitimate offspring that he also kicked in stipends for housing and food on top of the tuition.

Jesse's meeting Patty was your typical fairytale: Emotionally disturbed boy obsessed with a fictional movie character's fascination with an even more emotionally disturbed poet meets emotionally needy trailer park lawyer and procreation professional.

From his newly acquired obsession with the work of Edgar Alan, Jesse had turned to trying his own hand at poetry. Having never read any poetry besides that of Edgar Alan, and having no literary interests outside of this obsession, Jesse's "original" creations read as exactly what they were: poorly executed plagiarism.

Those who can't do, teach. Those who can't teach, become scholars.

Jesse's peculiar ability to not only quote liberally the works of Edgar Alan, but to communicate in everyday life exclusively in quotation of the poet, earned him a job as the literary critic for the local newspaper. Just as Jesse spoke only in quotes, his reviews were written exclusively in quotation of the morbid master. His sick and twisted obsession was a novelty to those readers who understood how truly bad his writing was. Those who longed to see themselves as victims of "the man" and "the system," those who strove to be intellectually superior, failed to recognize the absurdity of Jesse's condition. Those poor damned souls idolized Jesse's plagiarism of Edgar Alan with the same devout reverence with which Jesse obsessed over the poet himself.

I don't know which category Patty fell under. I don't know if she was amused by Jesse's affliction or if she sided with those who saw him as touched by God. What I do know is that she sought him out, frequenting poetry reading after Godawful poetry reading at coffeehouses and bookstores throughout the city.

If there was a poetry reading, Jesse was most assuredly there in all his forlorn glory, his tight black shirt stretched over the emaciated frame achieved on a diet of coffee and cigarettes. Black pants and boots hid the unearthly white skin that had long forgotten the effects of the sun. A long black leather trench coat defied summer heat, or noticeably disappeared from the ensemble in winter when such protection would be warranted by those not fixated on doing the inexplicable. And where Jesse went, so did his followers.

In the darkest corner of the rear of whatever hall might be host to the reading, Jesse would sit in sullen silence, his head hanging, his unkempt hair falling forward. There always was a dark corner, of course. If a store or restaurant desired Jesse's presence, it had to be dark. And there was no such thing as a poetry reading without the presence of the sad Crow offspring. Why bother?

Nobody sat with Jesse, although he was the focus of those in attendance. Some might feign interest in the poet whose name had been advertised, but who was not the attraction for coming. There were the usuals, the familiar faces. They shared a common enthrallment with the brooding critic, saw each other at every event, but never talked with each other. The awkward silence between them was part of the ambiance, the attraction. It paralleled the screaming, vicious silence that radiated from the darkest corner towards the speaking poet.

People didn't come for the poet. They came for the silence. They came for the awkward anticipation, the wonder of if it would be broken. Not just broken, but shattered. Not cracked, but destroyed.

Jesse did not watch the reader, the poet, he'd come to recount in his unique, if not original, writer's voice to his reading audience. I doubt sincerely if he even heard the words being spoken from the lone spot of light at the front of the room.

It was his coffee that he watched. When hot, the steam would billow as if smoke from a cigarette. When cold, the dark brew lay still – always black, its bleak murky color and harsh, okra taste never tainted by such pleasantries as sweetener or milk. Perhaps that's why he stared at it so long, for hours, because of the taste. Prior to his rebirth as the ambassador of doom, Jesse had never been able to touch coffee unless it was heavily disguised with the kinds of sugary, milky flavors and additives that any good Poe inspired ghoul would never ingest.

Finally it would happen – the performance that all had come to see. The poet had served his purpose; he was, of course, merely the opening act for the unadvertised headliner.

From the dark of his table, in the dark of the room, Jesse would mumble a quotation of misery to describe his distaste of the poet's work. The opinion was always of distaste and contempt, how could it not be? The self-professed poet on display was not speaking the words of Edgar Alan, the only true writer of any literary worth, but the blasphemy of a hack amateur who had dared lay claim to the title of poet, a title reserved only for the father of *The Raven*.

The room, already hushed, would transition to a state so quiet that if such a thing as negative sound were possible, it surely would be in effect. Those close enough to the darkest corner may have been lucky enough to hear, if not decipher, the initial mumbling of the critic. The room would strain to hear, as if continued silence might bring back the words that had escaped them before.

As the silence peaked, almost physical in its overwhelming presence in the room, the lone chair in the darkest corner would push back from the table. The solitary man so carefully dressed as to appear to have dressed with no thought of audience or season, would stand. With all eyes upon him, in a voice clear yet somber, he would repeat his critique.

"Those who dream by day are cognizant of many things which escape those who dream only by night," he might say if the poet's work had been too cheery.

"Three eloquent words oft uttered in the hearing of poets, by poets- as the name is a poet's, too. Its letters, although naturally lying like the knight Pinto- Mendez Ferdinando- still form a synonym for Truth- Cease trying! You will not read the riddle, though you do the best you can do," he might say if the work had been truly bad, not even needing a comparison to the late Poe to be recognized as poor.

"I have no time to dote or dream. You call it hope - that fire of fire! It is but agony of desire. If I can hope – oh God, I can! Its fount is holier - more divine. I would not call thee fool, but such is not a gift of thine," he might say if the poet had dared to create passages that someone not so dedicated to the work of the master might have actually been impressed with.

And then Jesse would be gone. His wisdom had been spoken. His audience had been fulfilled. His presence was no longer needed. He would write his full review in private. To stay might invite conversation, and then he would no longer be alone. Being alone was what defined him. So quoth the Raven, "Nevermore."

Patty didn't run into Jesse at one of the poetry readings. Jesse shunned attention from his fans. They were his fans because he refused their camaraderie; by welcoming it, he would no longer be what they desired. That's what it came down to, a desire to be desired. He had no friends. He had no family. Either through death or relocation, he'd lost everyone who mattered. He wanted to be wanted, even if that meant pretending that he didn't.

Patty ran into Jesse outside of one of the poetry readings. She literally ran into him. Well, her car did. She just happened to be driving it.

Jesse never looked when he crossed the street. He didn't cross at the corner or obey signals. He actively avoided them, would go out of his way to cross in the middle of the street rather than use a designated crosswalk.

It was part of his Crow-disciple image. To fear death was to invite death, allow it to control you until it grew bored of toying with you and ended the charade of life. To live without fear, to not just ignore but to actively challenge the reaper was to achieve immortality. Immortality not meaning to live forever, but to not be afraid to truly live.

If you ask me it was all bullshit. Then again, I thought dressing in leather during the summer, going around half naked in the winter, and speaking only the words of a dead man was kind of a bullshit way to live in general.

Anyway, Jesse made a habit of walking out into the middle of traffic to cross the street. Usually this resulted in some combination of horns honking, tires screeching, angry drivers yelling, and accidents left in his wake. This particular evening, the man dressed in black crossing the unlit street with no regard to traffic resulted in the man in black lying face down in the street after being struck by a law student looking for a parking space for a poetry reading she was running late for.

Despite his best "I don't need help" martyr routine, Jesse was down for the count and consented to allow the young law student to escort him into a nearby café to collect himself. It's not that Jesse was actually badly injured, since to be truthful Patty hadn't been driving very fast. But despite his lone wolf emulation of an invincible comic book character, Jesse has never been the most rugged individual. Let's put it this way: in high school, he was the guy making fun of the football players to cover his fear of actually getting out there and playing himself.

On the other hand, if Jesse had known the driver had been on her way to witness his lone Crow poetry act, he never would have accepted her help. Even with broken bones, internal bleeding, or one of those obnoxious hang nails that are more irritating than most severe injuries, he would have refused her help if he had known she was a groupie. But I will say that Patty is not a stupid girl. She knew that if Jesse knew she was a fan he wouldn't have had anything to do with her. Quiet frankly, I wouldn't be surprised if she might have been running late for that poetry reading on purpose.

No matter if Patty's heroine to the fallen loner, the one soul that could recognize the wall around his heart was made of fragile glass and not harden stone, was all an act, partially an act, or truly sincere – he fell for it all the same.

Carlos, the father of Patty's second child, lived in Las Vegas. He'd run off with his secretary when Patty was 8 months pregnant. He just didn't come home from work one day – until then, he too had been living in the extended-family household of interconnected trailer homes that Patty still called her rent-free home. A week or two later, Patty got a postcard explaining his departure. Just over a year had gone by when Patty met Jesse.

Within days of their meeting, Jesse was a part of the trailer family. "You should just give up your apartment and pay us a little rent," suggested Patty's mother.

Taylor, a precious and precocious three year old, timidly asked, "Will you be my daddy?" Patty had run away from her first husband, Taylor's father, when he'd put her head through the sheet rock wall of their Army base home. Taylor hadn't had a father since. Carlos, the father of his half brother Christian, had filled that role for Taylor to the extent that he took the kid to the men's room at restaurants. But that was about it. When Taylor had asked

Carlos to be his daddy, the request was met with a hasty, "Don't call me that."

Jesse, also the son of an absentee father, saw himself in Taylor – a kid wanting to be loved. Sometimes out of the blue, little Taylor with his golden tan and dancing blue eyes would stop in the middle of his games to run over to Jesse, wrap his arms around him, and say with heartfelt sincerity, "I love you so much!" He'd hold the hug for a moment and then resume playing.

He was a big kid; tall, not fat. And amazingly bright. He'd been potty trained since he was barely two. "I was tired of changing diapers," explained Patty of the hours she kept Taylor sitting on his training seat at such a young age, punishing him if he soiled a diaper and praising him if he used the potty. At three years old he could already read short sentences. The Speak and Spell that Jesse bought him was his favorite toy, especially since his "daddy" gave it to him.

Christian was an utter contrast to his half brother. In terms of appearance, Patty had very recessive genes, it seemed. Taylor had inherited all of his father's golden-boy good looks; Christian's father hadn't stood more than five foot five, and there was no questioning his Mexican heritage. Where Taylor was tall for his age, Christian was abnormally short. Where Taylor was skinny, Christian was fat – known to the family as Chunk. Where Taylor filled each room with a glow of happiness, Christian's constant tantrums only gave way to laughter when he was hitting other children. It was an evil laugh, more evil than a child should be able to create. "Satan Spawn," Patty sometimes joked about her little Chunk.

Yet, Patty loved Christian most. It was painfully clear. It was probably also the reason that Taylor worked so hard to please everyone and had latched onto Jesse so quickly – to be wanted.

What Patty never got over was that Chunk's father had left her. She'd always been the one to leave a relationship, but Carlos had left her. In her heart the relationship had never been resolved because she hadn't been the one in control. So she clung to Christian, coddled her link to the unresolved relationship. Of course she didn't tell Jesse this. Jesse was the love of her life, she said.

Shortly after they'd begun dating, Patty asked Jesse to go to Las Vegas with her. Carlos and his secretary/fiancée were living with his mother. Chunk's grandmother wanted to see him, wanted Carlos to see him.

At first Jesse was not going to go. "I can't afford a hotel on my own," explained Patty. "If you don't come then I'll have to stay in the house with Carlos and that would be really awkward." Jesse agreed to go.

Patty definitely knew her way around dollar signs. That's what men were to her, expense accounts with legs. The first month of dating, Jesse rang up over a thousand dollars on meals for his little ready-made family. Individually, meals out didn't register as big expenses. But at the end of the month, they really add up.

Las Vegas was an interesting trip for Jesse. The hustle and bustle of neon lights and crowded rooms was a dramatic contrast to the Poe-inspired environment Jesse had so carefully cultivated. Actually, the loner-king image had started to fade. It's rather hard to maintain a sense of being alone when you spend every moment with a girlfriend and two children, and you practically live with them and all their relatives in cramped corners.

They dropped Chunk off with his father and then checked into their hotel. The odd thing about Vegas hotel rooms is that they pretty much suck. The idea is to make you want to not stay in your room, because if you are in your room then you're not gambling and losing your retirement fund at the tables. The rooms are always dark, with bad lighting. And there are no clocks – that way if you wake up at 2 A.M. with a hankering to play slots, you don't look at the clock and say "Oh, it's 2 A.M., I should probably go back to sleep."

Rather then hang around the dreary room, Patty and Jesse took in dinner. Patty had a talent for spending Jesse's money, and she managed to secure reservations at one of the swankier eateries – the kind of place where you don't put your napkin in your lap, the waiter does it for you. Such places, where the calligraphy on the hand-written menus doesn't include the prices, charge so grandly for their services that they will not hesitate to pander to customers with offerings of complementary bottles of wine as a gesture of apology for the simplest indiscretions.

Jesse and Patty were made to wait 3-minutes past their reservation time before being shown to their private booth. How could they pass up the fine champagne offered for the inconvenience of waiting such an egregious length of time?

The events of the evening are a bit hazy for Jesse. According to the crumpled receipts in his pockets, the couple had ordered and presumably shared an additional three bottles of the bubbling nectar at the restaurant. Because Jesse detested seafood, it was probable that Patty had been the one to enjoy the lobster dinner. Jesse himself apparently had consumed a steak more expensive than he thought possible, until a call to the restaurant confirmed that a three-figure steak did in fact exist. For such a price, he certainly hoped he'd enjoyed it.

The joy of discovery of festivities lost in the fog of inebriation was not over for Jesse. More credit card receipts revealed that Jesse and his lovely companion had enjoyed their beverages at the restaurant so much, they'd ventured to a nightclub and sampled unimaginable concoctions of strong and flavorful spirits.

Perhaps it was these spirits that both inspired the action and later blocked out the memory of the next purchase Jesse was able to decipher from the cryptic credit card vouchers. An inspection of his companion who lay sleeping beside him confirmed the purchase. Although not clothed, Patty's sleeping form was not entirely naked. On her hand, the left one, three fingers away from the thumb, on a digit aptly referred to as "the ring finger," was just such a sparkling, diamond adornment. Now Jesse really hoped he'd enjoyed his steak.

acting harmless

Being an actor is not like being a track and field athlete. In a race, the fastest person wins. In acting, the best person for a role isn't necessarily going to get it. Going back to the race analogy, it would be like having 10 of the best conditioned athletes in the world on the starting line and the judges run up into the stands and hand the gold medal to a middle aged smoker.

There are no rules in acting. A theater in Ohio may cast the TV weatherman as Hamlet, not because he's any good but because people will come see him. Too bad for all those guys in tights who have been studying their whole lives for the chance to play that role.

I love performing. I really do. But let's face it: I never got cast because I was a good actor. I got cast because I was good looking and for the most part I was a harmless actor.

Kevin Costner is a harmless actor. As long as he's playing Kevin Costner, or a character that is like Kevin Costner, he's fine. If he is asked to play a character that isn't Kevin Costner, if he's actually asked to act and not just say lines, well then you get *Water World*.

I was cast in the television movie adaptation of William Inge's *Picnic* because I look good with my shirt off. Plain and simple, that's what it came down to.

The fact is the character of Hal falls right into my harmless acting repertoire. He's enough like me that as long as I just say the lines and don't think about it, I'm Hal. He's a guy who gets by on his looks, who doesn't look for trouble but can't seem to outrun it, and who tends to stir things up when he hits town. Pretty much, it's me. So, if I had just kept with my harmless acting approach I would have done just fine.

But for some reason I felt compelled to try do better than just harmless acting. I was playing the lead in a Pulitzer Prize winner. Paul Newman had played the role on stage. William Holden had played the character in the movies. It's considered one of the greatest plays in American history.

With that legacy to live up to, I decided for *Picnic* I needed to become an *actor* rather than just a TV star. Hey, Marilyn Monroe had done it when she did *Bus Stop*. She flew to New York and worked with Lee Strasberg or whoever that method acting guy was.

Of course we're talking TV movie of the week here, not major motion picture. And I've never had near the clout of a Marilyn Monroe. Besides, for all my good intentions I don't think I was quite dedicated enough to go live in New York for weeks or months or however long it is might take to learn how to touch my inner child and cry on cue by drawing on sensory memory. That all sounds nice and technical, but you know what? You can cry on cue by pulling out leg hairs.

Instead of doing the whole New York, hard work, method acting thing, I got a private tutor in LA. We'd do coffee in Malibu and she'd talk to me about "my craft" and my body being my instrument. And I'd try to listen.

It's kind of like those instruction manuals for appliances though. They started off in Japanese, then got translated to Spanish, and then from Spanish into English. In the end, the words are all English, but they don't necessarily make sense or tell you how to work the appliance.

Lara, my coach, had studied under someone who had studied method acting. And now I was getting the crash course from her. But the message was kind of watered down and out of sequence by the time it got to me. Plus I'm not that great of a student. We'd usually end back at Lara's, screwing. Come to think of it, the sex was probably the only appropriate research I did with Lara for *Picnic*. Everything else she "taught" me in her beachfront café lectures contributed to creating the worst performance of my career.

If Lara sounds two-dimensional I'm doing her justice because she is probably the most one-dimensional person I've ever met. In LA, that's saying something.

Nonetheless, I went into production on *Picnic* convinced by Lara's tutoring that I could act. Really act.

There's an old adage that Shakespeare done well is amazing to watch, while Shakespeare done poorly is painful to watch. I now know that as a harmless actor, I'm agreeable to watch. As an *actor*-actor, I'm painful to watch. It is painful to watch someone trying so hard and failing so miserably. At least with harmless acting it's not painful when the actor fails because they weren't trying too hard.

I remember a story Barry Williams told about the time he showed up stoned on *The Brady Bunch* set. The scene was typical Brady. Barry's character Greg is in the driveway with his bike and says a few harmless words. Being stoned, though, Barry decided he was going to be Master Thespian and put great meaning into the words. After a few embarrassing takes, someone pulled him aside and told him to get his shit together. He cooled the Master Thespian act real quick and turned in a nice meaningless Greg Brady standard.

I wasn't stoned when I rolled into Corpus Christi, Texas to start filming. But I did have the whole Master Thespian concept down. I'd even arranged for Lara to be hired on by the network as my on-set acting coach. She had a private little chair next to the director where she could watch my performance and call me over to receive her little critiques – tell me how wonderful I was doing, tell me how to adjust my instrument. She'd also turn from time to time to tell the director he was a bore and lacked creative vision if he grumbled anything about my performance.

Lara lasted exactly one day on the set. When she and I showed up on the lot for the second day of filming, Don – one of the assistant directors – pulled me to the side and told me the director didn't want Lara on the set. Don was the likable A.D., the guy who didn't know anything about film or television but was really good at making everyone feel good. Thus, he was also very good at getting rid of problems. He's the guy the director sends to get rid of pain-in-the-ass acting coaches because Don can do it diplomatically whereas anyone else would be an asshole.

So, there's Don munching on his craft-services donut and drinking from his styrofoam cup of coffee, telling me with a good old boy grin that he likes Lara just fine and her input is obviously so valuable, but for insurance reasons she can't be on the set anymore. You couldn't help but like Don. Unless of course you were Lara and being told you couldn't be on the set.

"Bullshit," Lara said. She had her Starbucks French blend, double latté and high fiber cranberry-almond muffin in her hands.

"He doesn't work without me," she continued, motioning at no-mind-of-his-own me like a stage mother to a child star. "He needs me."

Don chewed on his donut and smiled that agreeable smile of his – the one that says, "I know exactly what you mean" no matter what the fuck he really is thinking inside.

"I know exactly what you mean," he said, slipping a twinkle eyed wink to me at the same time – as if to say "I'm appeasing your friend here, I know you're a good actor" to me while at the same time telling her "I know he needs you, but my hands are tied." Don was a master.

The director on the shoot wasn't into diplomacy, which is why Don was sent to ditch Lara and hopefully save my performance from being one of the worst in the history of movies of the week. The director, though, also wasn't into patience. He was ready to start filming and wanted Lara gone, Don and his diplomacy be damned. He lumbered over to us in his corduroy splendor, wiping

106

the dabs of perpetual fat-man sweat from underneath the brim of his ever-present baseball cap that concealed his ever-growing bald spot.

"You're out of here, honey," he said in a blunt New York accent, pointing to Lara with a pudgy finger. In the same breath he turned to me, pointed with the same pudgy finger, and told me to get to wardrobe.

Lara's holier-than-thou, highbrow attitude shot her nose about 3 inches higher in the air as she grabbed my arm. "Come on dear, we'll go wait in the hotel until they're ready to act like professionals."

Lara's suggested threat didn't faze the director. I wish I could remember his name. Anyway, he ignored her completely. He looked me in the eye and put it to me point blank, "She's fucking up your performance. She goes and you go with her, and we'll get Antonio Sabato Jr. Or she goes and you stay and we make a movie. Either way she goes. Your choice."

Lara immediately went into a tirade about how we wouldn't stand for this kind of treatment, how my contract had guarantees, and other crap like that. She shut up though when I told her she was fired. She was just kind of standing there with her mouth gaping – maybe even in midsentence – as I headed to wardrobe.

I didn't win an Emmy for *Picnic*. I wasn't even nominated. But I ended up doing a pretty harmless job.

bus fare

When I was fourteen years old I met my mentor, Corey. He was a producer at the local Denver affiliate of one of the big three networks, back when there were just three main networks. Corey was an articulate, highly professional black man, probably around 30. I was at the library reading a copy of *BackStage Magazine,* checking out the audition notices. He came up to me, made note of what I was reading and asked if I was an actor. Once I introduced myself, he knew right away who I was and had seen some of my theatre work around town. He said it was a waste that I was doing theatre in a small town like Denver, and that I should be working in television. He gave me his card and said to give him a call.

Corey and I struck up a mentor/student type of relationship. I knew it wasn't all him just being nice. He was looking to make money and produce hit shows, and he was grooming me to be a star so he could make money. I had no problem with that. He got me on the list at fancy parties to hobnob with the right people. He always sang my praises to the big wigs at these things, told them I was going to be the next big thing. He got me into movie premiers. I was meeting all the right people.

One night he called up and said he'd pitched me to the network executives in LA for a new sitcom and they were flying out to meet me. They wanted me down at the studio the next day. He asked me to come over to his apartment so he could prepare me for the meeting. Of course I went. Remember, I was just a teenager, so I had to have my Dad drop me off. But he'd met

Corey before. He just said to call when I was ready to get picked up.

Corey had the television on when I got there, and as we talked and he filled me in on what to expect the next day, he'd occasionally make reference to the people on the television. Arsenio Hall came on the screen and Corey claimed Arsenio only got his TV deal because he had a relationship with a producer with a lot of power. Sarah Jessica Parker came on and Corey told me a story about her supposedly using the casting couch to break into show business when she was my age. We talked a little more and suddenly Corey had his hand on my thigh.

At first I thought it was just one of those buddy things people do. But he didn't take his hand away; he left it there. It felt like time was slowing down as I got more and more uncomfortable. Then his hand was running up and down my leg. Then he was leaning in towards me.

"You know what I want," he whispered. "I have power. I can make things happen for you."

I should have just left, but I wanted so bad to be a star. But I also wasn't willing to do what he wanted. I picked up his hand and moved it away from me. He got really angry.

"Don't be a little girl," he said.

He tried to kiss me and I moved out of the way and off of the couch.

"Don't fuck this up," he warned. "I can get you the deal, but only if you play nice. Now come sit down. You can close your eyes and think about a girl."

I didn't want to admit this was happening. I tried to reason with him.

"Corey, I thought you were my friend," I said. I can still hear the pleading in my voice.

He was done trying to sweet talk me into what he wanted.

"You come here or the deal is off. You'll never work again," he threatened.

I was terrified. I tried to open the door to run, but my hands were shaking so hard I couldn't get the handle to turn. Then I finally did, but the security chain was still latched so I couldn't get the door all the way open.

I felt Corey's breath on my neck, his hand stroking my shoulder as I struggled to get the chain lock undone. I was trembling so hard I couldn't even think, but somehow I got the door open and I ran. I tried the elevator button but it seemed like an eternity. I could see Corey coming down the hall after me. He was walking so calm and relaxed. He'd taken his time putting on his trench coat.

I bolted down the fire stairs. I ran all the flights down and out onto the street. I ran and ran, my heart racing. I could hear it beating. The feeling thundered through my whole body with every beat. Thump Thump. Thump Thump. I was hysterical. I couldn't even breathe. My lungs hurt from running while not able to breathe. I looked behind me, and there was Corey emerging from his apartment building – walking after me as calm and cool as ever.

I saw a bus approaching the next corner. I didn't know where the bus was going. I didn't care. I ran and ran, scared to death that I wouldn't make it to the bus and Corey would catch me. My legs hurt. My lungs hurt. I could hardly see because of the tears streaming down my face. But I caught it. I don't know how, but I got on that bus.

My hands were shaking so hard I couldn't get the change out of my pocket to pay my fare. The driver just sat there waiting for me to pay. I glanced out the door and there was Corey walking along so calm towards the bus – but his eyes fixed on me with this cold mix of amusement and hatred, taunting me, telling me he was going to get me. The driver's voice was far away, like I was hearing him through water, as he asked if I was going to pay or get off the bus.

I turned and looked at the driver but couldn't talk, couldn't explain what was happening. All I could muster was a feeble "Please."

I don't know if it was the terror in my eyes or the tears on my face or my shaking hands dropping coins on the floor of the bus or if they saw that same look in Corey's eyes as he neared the bus, but someone behind me reached over and deposited money in the fare box. "There you go son, it's okay" the other passenger said with a gentle hand on my shoulder. And the driver closed the doors and pulled away, leaving Corey staring at me through the door with those eyes.

Obviously I didn't get that series. I didn't even get the meeting. I doubt I would have been able to go had they sent the car as promised. I was a wreck. I blamed myself for being in that situation. I replayed it over and over trying to figure out some way I could have not had that happen – if I had said I couldn't have made it to Corey's that night, then he wouldn't have been able to try to force himself on me and I would have had my series – right? He would still be my friend then, right? So it was my fault for having gone to his house, right? It's all my fault, right?

I've spent a lifetime having people view me purely as a sex object. I am so fearful that people will tell me they love me when all they want is sex. But at the same time if they don't tell me I'm sexy, then I think I'm not worthy and they're going to leave me for someone better. I think that's why my fantasy isn't about making love to a woman, but to lay naked together – to be admired so I'd feel sexy but without expectations so I'd feel loved.

mommy dearest

When I refer to my biological mother I always say that I never *really* knew her, but I did know her. I met her when I was 15 years old.

When I say my "biological mother," it sounds like I had a figurative mother by comparison. I didn't. There really is no need to differentiate my biological mother from anyone else. I guess I just refer to her that way to point out that all she was as a mother was biological, nothing more. Not that I didn't want something more. Whether I have admitted it to others or even to myself, I have always longed for a mother. Unfortunately, we don't choose our parents.

It was no coincidence my father and I had ended up in Denver. It was where I was born, the first place my father had moved after college. He idealizes the city; he always has.

My father had taken the job in New York after I was born for the money because of the medical bills. But he had applied for every transfer opportunity he could to get back to Denver. Thanks to *Feed & Supplements*, we made our grand return, but he never mentioned it was where my biological mother lived as well.

Scanning the local paper one morning as a teenager I came across my mother's name. She was listed in the police blotter, arrested for drunk driving. Conveniently the mention came along with an address, as did all those individuals mentioned in the police blotter. Apparently the rule of innocent until proven guilty doesn't have any protective clauses about privacy.

I called information for her number. Fifteen is the age when you can do things like call information for the phone number of the biological mother you've never met, only read about in the police blotter of the local paper. Younger than fifteen and you don't really understand how to go about tracking her down; you don't understand that it is really as simple as a phone call. Older than fifteen and cynicism has started to set in, you doubt if you should track down someone who has been nothing to you. But at fifteen, you don't even think; you just pick up the phone and call. And at fifteen, when information doesn't have a listing for your mother, you just hop on the bus to the address listed in the paper.

It wasn't that she had an unlisted number, it turns out. She had a tendency to forget to pay bills. She hadn't had a phone in years. No phone company would provide her service.

My first impulsive trip across town to meet my mother was not an emotional, tear-filled event. From the front window of her trailer I could see her on a lounge chair, bottle in her hand. Neither my knocking at the door, or the resultant barking of her dog, "Doorbell," was enough to wake her from her stupor. She was passed out for the day, at one o'clock in the afternoon. Visiting hours were over.

We officially met on my second visit to the trailer she had inherited from her father. One might think that finding an individual passed out drunk at one o'clock in the afternoon would mean you should arrive earlier in the day to ensure an awake if not alert host. Having grown up under the roof of a functionally alcoholic father, I knew better than this. When drinking begins with waking, the morning window of sobriety is very narrow indeed. However, most drunks will get their afternoon siesta over with by about 7 PM so they can be wide awake and ready to drink the night away.

Mommy dearest didn't seem too surprised to see me. Maybe someone in the trailer park had told her I'd been by the other day. I doubt it. I think she just had that level of alcohol in her where nothing could be a surprise. "There's a 7-foot tall half-fish, half-monster eating the neighbor." "Ahh, that's nice. I think I'll have another drink."

I honestly don't even remember having to introduce myself, explain who I was. I'm sure I did. But whatever explanation was necessary, it couldn't have been too in-depth. There was no hug or kisses, anger, sadness, happiness, or elation. Her welcome was a casual "come in" as she returned to her lounge chair perch in front of the TV, fetching cocktails for herself and her 15-year-old guest.

In most homes, fetching a drink involves going to the kitchen. My mother had done away with such unnecessary travel. It was actually a system devised by her father, which she had inherited along with the trailer.

The living room was truly that: where she lived. I'm sure the trailer had bedrooms in the back, but they were long forgotten. Life in the trailer revolved around a reclining lounge chair that served both as a place to sit when upright and a place to sleep when reclined. The television, which was never turned off, sat directly in front of the chair. And to the immediate right, within reaching distance of the captain's chair, was the mini refrigerator – always well stocked.

She handed me a wine cooler, took her seat, and resumed watching whatever mindless prime-time fluff was on the television. There was no "you must be wondering about me" or "tell me about yourself" exchange. I was simply there.

The living room was laid out for optimum convenience for its single resident, but offered little concession to visitors. I accepted the drink and, after an awkward pause, retrieved a stool from the kitchen to sit on. We talked during commercials, only during commercials. If she was in midsentence when her program came back on, she'd simply stop talking. Of course the unfinished thought would be long forgotten by the next commercial break.

With my father being so nondescript, so blend into the crowd average, I guess I figured my mother would have been a beauty, the one responsible for my own looks. If at one time she had been of fair and delicate features, that time was long ago and well forgotten. Left to my best guess, I would wager my parents are proof-positive that recessive genes in two unremarkable individuals can result in a child that is all either of them was not.

In her kitchen, proof of its forgotten purpose resided on the stovetop. In a small pot on the range was a stuffed bunny. It was not a formerly live bunny that had been stuffed for cooking. It was not a formerly live bunny that had been stuffed for display. It was a child's toy stuffed animal, sitting in a pot on the stove.

Apparently during her father's late years, his mind had degenerated to something like that of a child. The bunny was his toy that he clung to as he sat waiting to die each day in the lounge chair in front of the television, no longer needing drink to impair his faculties. By then he simply drank out of habit.

When my mother was feeling particularly cruel, inspired by flashbacks of the abuse she'd suffered at his hands in her childhood, she would steal bunny away from the old man with the child's brain. She would taunt him with it, holding it out of his reach while he clawed the air and cried for its return.

When dinnertime would roll around and my grandfather still sat whimpering over his loss, mommy dearest would emerge from the kitchen and ask the old man if he was hungry. Again she would tease what was left of his mind, working him into a hyper excited state, jumping up and down in his seat in anticipation of some sort of tasty delight. Pulling the top off of the serving pot, his daughter would cackle in wicked joy as his eyes discovered not food to eat, but his lone toy and friend crammed inside. "Bunny stew!" my mother would laugh over and over; her father screeching in terror, yanking the toy from the pot and cradling it to his chest.

That's how I got to know my mother. Sound bytes of information during commercial breaks. Most of her stories were about her sexual escapades, both willing and non. Not exactly the most ideal subject matter through which a child should learn about his parent.

"Do you consider the age you lose your virginity to be the first time you have sex or the first time you willingly have sex?" she asked me in our very first commercial break together. She proceeded to tell me about how she was molested as a child and by which family members. In our next commercial break I got to hear of her first rape.

I should probably mention that my mother was a heroin addict. That started long after she got pregnant with me. I think she had me when she was nineteen. That's a guess, but I think I'm close.

Mother dearest started using when she was in her late twenties, specifically when she hooked up with Boogie. Boogie was a scummy Mexican truck driver who had dreams of being a biker, that's how my mother described him. The funny thing is, she had this adoration in her eye when she said that. Not just in her eye, but in the way she said the words. It's as if being scummy was what was good about him. Maybe that was the attraction.

Boogie, whose real name wasn't much better – Hector Hernandez – was not a good lover, my mother also shared with me. He was, she said, under-endowed.

"Even if it was true that size doesn't matter, Boogie didn't know how to use what he did have," she said with an admiration that contradicted the context of what she said. "Boogie's style was to go real fast and sleep when it's over."

Apparently, he also wet the bed. Mother blamed his little bladder problem on his truck driving: the long bumpy trips ravaged his kidneys. If it was kidneys, it couldn't have been his alcoholism that ravaged them, could it? Anyway, mother became an expert midnight mattress flipper on account of Boogie's little leakage problem.

Boogie treated my mother the way he treated all women. To him, life was there for his benefit; he had no sense of consequence, no sense of responsibility, and certainly no sense of others. Ma was Boogie's date to his own wedding.

At 5'7", he wasn't a tall man. And, heroin being the miracle diet that it is, he weighed in at a bone-skinny 130 pounds.

What is it about men and women and their weight? Men always weigh an even amount, at least some derivative of five. You never meet a guy who tells you he weighs 172 pounds. He either weighs 170 or 175. Chicks, on the other hand, always sell themselves at a very specific weight: 121-1/2, or something like that. Even when they are lying about their weight, like the fat girls do on their driver's licenses, they drop it down to 153 instead of 250. I believe it may be a fact that no female driver's license in history has ever been issued with a weight over 172 pounds. I guess I must be a really bad judge of size because I could swear some of the girls I've seen with 141 pounds listed on their license looked like they were pushing 300 pounds.

Boogie was not only short and scrawny, according to my mother, there just wasn't anything physically attractive about him. Normally on a person there's at least one feature you can point to as being attractive, or at least their best. Finding a best on Boogie was choosing the least of far more than two evils.

Boogie had this odd, horse-like extended face. Not only did he have bad skin, but he was unable to grow any kind of full facial hair, so he sported these tufts of weak-looking wisps in the spots where they would grow. He was like the bald guys who try to comb their hair over the bald spot. Boogie, I guess, hoped that by plastering the long wisps of facial hair over the barren portions of his face, it'd somehow give the impression he had real facial hair.

I never met Boogie, so I can't say with all certainty that he stank. But given that he rarely bathed, spent long hours riding cooped up in a truck, owned a total of two pairs of pants and three shirts but no washing machine, and that he peed himself in his sleep, I figure it's a pretty safe bet his odor wasn't his best quality either.

Mother's best friend actually also dated Boogie, at the same time that my mother was dating him, which was at the same time he was in the process of marrying someone else. For being an unattractive man with bad hygiene and no bedroom skills to speak of, Boogie sure had his pick of the ladies. My mother is evidence that some women become conditioned to subconsciously hunger for abuse. I find that so sad.

From the patchwork of stories I recall, my mother had come to live with her father in his final year or two. She was there to care for him as he died because it was a family responsibility and her brothers hadn't stepped up to the plate. Odd to hear a delinquent mother like her talk emphatically about family responsibility. But I didn't argue the point, for fear of alienating her and cutting short the brief conversations that were as close to mothering as she would ever offer.

What was so odd about her caring for the old man in his later years, of sharing the same roof, was that the only other stories she told about him were about how he molested her.

Her first sexual contact was as a child when her father molested her. Next came getting raped by a boy she thought was her friend at the age of 13. At the age of 16, she was gang raped by three boys from her school behind a grocery store. She had thought she was the luckiest girl in the world when three popular upperclassman had volunteered to walk her home.

Some people who are sexually assaulted become scared of sex; others have their self esteem so shattered that they become sexual addicts. My mother was a sexual addict.

I think there are people who have been so abused in their lives, have become so accustomed to it, that they don't know how to interact with others without abuse. If they're not receiving the abuse, then they assume the role of the abuser, just so someone is getting abused.

I didn't get to know my mother well. I only visited a few times before I just couldn't take it anymore. But I think she was like that, so used to abuse that she couldn't function without either being abused or abusing someone else.

who wants to screw a celebrity?

Drugs can make you do some fucked up shit. That's not a new concept. Actually I don't think they become fucked up things until after you have sobered up. If you hit on the boss' wife one night after drinking too much at the office party, the next day when you wake up with that head-splitting, can't-move hangover you realize you did something fucked up.

However, if you continue drinking, never letting sobriety rear its evil head, you never realize you did anything fucked up. Hitting on the boss' wife not only seems like a wise move to have made, you'll probably call her up later that day and continue the courtship. Stay perpetually fucked up long enough and you'll probably score the girl and live in the boss's old house once the divorce is final. You'll become a kept man living off the now ex-boss' ex-wife's alimony. The key to never fucking up is never getting sober. Until then, all things are golden and you can do no wrong. Such was my entrance into the world of game shows.

I'd just finished the less than legendary straight-to-video classic *Rebel Fury*. The concept was that I would look cool on a motorcycle with my shirt off, wearing sunglasses on the video cover. Outside of that we had three days to shoot, lots of guns, wannabe bikers for extras, and chicks willing to do nudity for barely any money in hopes it would be their big break.

I didn't sleep the entire shoot. While the script was virtually nonexistent, thankfully the director didn't take himself too seriously. He's made a career of bouncing back and forth between doing these low budget "features," directing porn, and lecturing at some fine arts college. He knew we were making crap and pretty much his attitude was to get it done as quickly and cheaply as possible and spend whatever money was left over on coke – which he freely shared. It was good coke too.

Coke is a tricky drug. You get spoiled *really* easy. You run across a batch of good Colombian shit that they say is pure, which really means it's only 90% cut, and you're in heaven off a single line. Lick the mirror and you're waving down at God below you. You don't have to do more to feel good, but you do anyway.

But with coke you have to take what you can get. If you want shit, you want it then and there. There isn't a lot of forethought about it. I'm not talking junkie here, guys who need it all the time. I'm talking average Hollywood cokehead. You go a few weeks doing the "normal thing" – drinking, cruising, maybe even being sober. Then, you get the itch. When that itch comes, you page every dealer you have ever even heard of, every user you have ever pimped for a line, every person who might know someone who might know someone. At that point, you're not exactly a smart consumer.

So, sometimes you end up with shit. Who knows if there is even any coke in the batch? Maybe it's just vitamin C or something to give you enough of a false high to think there might be some trace of coke so you don't go off and pinch the dealer. With bad shit, you keep doing more and more in hopes that if you do enough it will get you to a place where you can at least see heaven, because you know it's not going to get you all the way there. But doing more doesn't get you any higher. Bad shit is bad shit. You just end up with a headache, a deviated septum, and a bitter taste in the back of your throat.

The *Rebel Fury* coke was good. I agreed to do my own stunts just so we wouldn't have to pay the stunt double and we could use the money to get another couple of grams.

Sometimes when you're high you wish you could sleep, you know your body is exhausted, you can feel the circles growing under your eyes, but your body won't let you. So you do more coke and the desire to sleep goes away for a while, or at least you don't pay too much attention to it. When it's really good coke, you never even think of sleeping – you just float there above the clouds. You're Superman and nothing can get you out of the sky because the earth has a yellow sun and you're from Krypton wearing tights.

Rebel Fury was yellow sun coke. I never even dreamed of sleep. We started turning day scenes into night scenes since we were all up anyway and knew the script sucked so bad there was nothing we could do to make it any worse.

And, of course there's the sniffle. To the untrained ear it sounds like you have a cold – your nose is stuffed up and running. But to anyone who has done coke, it doesn't sound like a cold at all. It's a very distinct sound. I can watch any film and tell you who's using right away.

When you first get booted out of the Promised Land of mainstream Hollywood, you vow that the straight-to-video flick is a one-shot deal to keep your name out there. Even though it's a thin script and you're surround by second-rate talent, people will see through it and realize your potential. You'll be back doing real work in no time.

Once you've resigned yourself to the fact that you're doing crap, accepted that it is a perpetual cycle with no way out, and realized that if you hook up with a like-minded director you can score some good drugs, you're praying for a sequel. Over the years we've done *Rebel Fury* sequels, prequels, and remakes – seven films in all so far, and counting.

After the first *Rebel Fury*, I was sitting around my house with the ever-present sniffles. The director had been cool enough to line me up with his source. I'd probably been flying for a week or so, with a sporadic stupor nap here and there, but nothing resembling real sleep.

The TV was on; it'd probably been on for days. But at the point I became aware of it, one of those *Who Wants to be a Millionaire?* type of shows was on. There was a whole slew of shows like that hitting the airwaves then. "Who Wants to Answer Stupid Trivia Questions Asked by a Talk Show Host?" "Who Wants to Marry a Guy They've Never

Met Because he Claims to be a Millionaire?" "Who Wants to Live on a Deserted Island and Eat Grubs and Become a Millionaire?"

It dawned on me that people will do anything for a chance at fame and fortune. They don't even have to get the fame and fortune; they just want to be tempted by it. So I thought of a game show for myself: *Who Wants to Screw a Celebrity?*

The premise is that you get to sleep with a celebrity, namely me. You don't get any money; you don't get any emotional commitment. But if you're the winner and you get to sleep with me, then there's a chance that you might get pregnant and be able to sue for far more child support than you'd get from the typical stiff you're letting use you. But that's not all! You also get the opportunity to try to sell your story to the tabloids and tell what a humiliating experience it was and how it makes you realize the awful sexist attitude Hollywood has against poor innocent women. And, you have the chance to further capitalize on your 15-minutes of fame by becoming a spokesperson for a weight loss clinic or by starring in straight-to-video movies. It had the same promise of a chance for fame and fortune that all those other lame-o game shows have, plus I'd be the star and get sex. It was brilliant – at least in my mind.

I called up my agent and left a blathering pitch of my idea on his voicemail. I'd signed with Steve right after my big time agent dumped me when I fell off the hot commodities list, so Steve was used to my coked up, 3 AM messages. At least I was decent enough to leave them on his voicemail at the office where he could play them for his staff as an example of why to stay away from drugs, rather than wake him up in the middle of the night at home like some used-to-be stars tend to do – the ones who are under the illusion that they still matter.

To his credit Steve didn't automatically dismiss my 3 AM blatherings as drug-induced nonsense. Yes they were drug induced, but some of my best ideas came in that state.

We once pitched a series to the networks that I came up with while on a 3-day coke binge. It was called *Heroes*, an offshoot of my childhood obsession with comic book superheroes and desire to become a real life superhero.

It took the approach of "what if superheroes were real?" Not in the comic book world, but in the real world where they had to deal with divorce and drug addiction and suicidal tendencies despite the inability to die.

One studio actually took the bait, but I walked out on the deal when they wouldn't let me star. I wasn't big enough any more, they said. I still gave a damn then. I hadn't gotten to the point of realizing nobody really cares who's in what. It's all about money. I was still naive enough to think I was due for another break, or that if one studio wanted the script, it wouldn't be hard to find another buyer.

This time Steve called and said the idea, the game show, was crap. I, however, still higher than Mt. Everest, was convinced that it was brilliant. I told Steve that he didn't know what he was talking about. Fearless and incapable of a bad idea, I started pitching the idea myself.

Of course, I had no idea how to pitch even a script, much less a mere concept. I didn't know any decision-makers personally. If Steve pitched one of my ideas to FOX or Paramount he'd tell me his contact liked the idea, he never said who the contact was. Or if he did, I didn't pay attention.

So, I just started calling studios – the front desk. I'd tell them who I was. If they happed to remember *Then Again* and if they also happened to believe it was actually me on the phone, some would take pity on me and let me talk to a low- level nobody.

A more sober person would have gotten discouraged after the first call or two. But I couldn't remember one minute from the next. A failure of a minute ago didn't exist.

Amazingly enough I talked to enough nobodies that I eventually started getting through to somebodies. Even more amazing, they actually liked the idea. They must have had the same dealer as me.

The thing about network executives is that they all have this overgrown kid mentality of wanting whatever the kid down the street wants – or, in this case, what the executive at the other network wants.

It doesn't matter how bad they think the idea is, if they hear that another network is interested, they convince themselves they want it too. I was suddenly in the middle of a bidding war for my game show. Little old agent Steve was more than happy to field the offers, no matter that he had told me my idea sucked. Money is money.

At first we were going to go with one of the big three networks. But once the legal department started getting involved, they wanted to change it into *Who Wants to Date a Celebrity?* That kind of takes the kick out of it, and it didn't guarantee me any sex. The lawyers claimed my original idea could be construed as prostitution or some crap like that. Like I cared.

So, we started looking at offers from cable. HBO and Showtime were pretty well established at doing independent series that the normal networks couldn't air, like *The Sopranos,* so a game show was a pretty obvious next step. And, of course, if they weren't ready to bite, we had your soft-core porn networks to turn to as well.

But *Who Wants to Be A Millionaire?* was losing popularity. And, let's face it, part of the whole public appeal of this little idea was it was taking that national obsession and adding sex to the mix. If the nation was no longer obsessed with the premise the show was based on, regardless of what you added it wasn't going to matter.

Steve was smart enough to realize that, and for once I was smart enough to listen. Maybe my supplier was starting to cut down on the purity of my coke and it was clearing my mind. When we saw the trend starting to fall away from Regis Philbin and his *Millionaire* game show, we took the highest offer on the table – some Canadian production company looking to syndicate the show a la *Baywatch* – and we walked away.

I think the show did eventually air in Europe. Maybe it was South America. Somewhere like that where David Hasselhoff is actually considered a singer. It was a cool idea though.

cyber hooker

When it comes to stocks and bonds, I've always let my broker handle investments. I make no claims to knowing the first thing about a portfolio. In my vocabulary, a portfolio is a bunch of pictures, so I leave investing to people whose inherent definition falls on the side of finance. However, I am responsible for the one investment that keeps me living in luxury instead of just living well.

Most of my brilliant ideas come to me in drunken or dope-induced stupors. That's not saying that the beer or coke influenced the decision. I just think I've spent so much time fucked up that it is only natural that ideas come to me in that state. Let's face it: if you have ten good ideas in your life and you spend 75% of your time fucked up, odds are that a good percentage of those ideas are going to happen when you're in that fucked-up state.

I don't remember exactly if it was a coke binge or a drinking binge. Probably a drinking binge, because the details are fuzzy. I tend to remember the coke events pretty vividly.

When I'm fucked up, I get obsessive about things. It's the addictive personality I have naturally, enhanced by a state where the boundaries of logic have all but disappeared.

When I'm drunk I have a tendency to cut my hair. I don't mean going somewhere to get my hair cut. I cut my hair. I have clippers in the bathroom under the sink, and the only time they ever come out is when I'm drunk. I've actually gotten pretty good at it. Still, it's always a little disconcerting when I wake up in the morning covered with little remnants of a 2 AM drunken hairdo. There's that moment of panic of realizing that I've done it yet again, and wondering if I did all right.

For a while I also got really obsessed with the Internet when I was fucked up. Sober, I couldn't care less about checking e-mail. No matter how private I try to keep my e-mail address, I always end up on someone's list of people to forward stupid jokes to. If a message says "Fwd" in front of it, I just erase it. But when I'm drunk, I have to go on the Internet. And I will stay on for hours with no purpose whatsoever.

It was during one of those Internet binges that I realized exactly what I was doing. I was on the Internet with no purpose, desperately trying to think of something to research so I could justify staying on. So I started re-reading old e-mails from friends.

There was an e-mail from Jesse asking what I wanted for my birthday. The date indicated he'd sent it months before. I guess I forgot my own birthday. Nonetheless, I sent Jesse a message back telling him to send me a hooker.

When I finally checked my e-mail again during my next stupor, Jesse had responded – quite promptly, it appeared. Apparently other people don't take two months to respond to messages. He politely informed me that since he'd never heard back from me, he'd sent me flowers, for which incidentally he'd never received a thank you.

I had to wonder if I'd given the flowers to one of the girls I was dating, passing them off as a thoughtful gift from me. Or maybe they were dried up somewhere in the house. Then again, being well aware that I wouldn't recall getting his gift anyway, Jesse might just have said he'd sent me a gift when he really hadn't.

At the end of his note, he added that he couldn't have got me a hooker anyway because you can't send them over the Internet. The next day I met with my accountant. Against his advisement I withdrew $10,000 from my savings, and I started a business.

Most actors start production companies. It's really just an ego thing. The studio pays for the office space. Secretaries field calls that go unreturned. And in the end the company's name is just stuck on a project that the studio develops anyway, and the star is obligated to do the project no matter how much they don't want to because they have to pay the studio back for setting up the production company.

That's most stars. I guess I was never a big enough star to warrant a vanity deal like that. The company I started had nothing to do with movies, nothing to do with television. It was *www.CyberHooker.net*. I was going to provide hookers over the Internet.

My friend Rick had been pestering me to buy into his strip club as a part owner. He'd never admit it, but Rick wanted me to buy in because he was losing money and he wanted a bankroll.

Rick claimed, and maybe he even believed, that he thought by having me as an investor it would draw people in. I don't know about that. Of the strip joints I've seen, most patrons are straight men. I don't see why they'd want to come see me sitting at the bar when there are naked women to look at on stage. During my peak, I'd gone through the phase of being overrun by fans on the street, in malls, in restaurants. But even in those days, I'd never drawn a crowd of autograph seekers in a strip club.

The reason Rick was losing money was that he was a bad businessman. That's why I suspect maybe he really did believe having a semi-celebrity hanging around would help business. It never occurred to him that since he was serving me free drinks and for the most part the girls let me have my pick of them in the back, I was already hanging out there quite a bit and it wasn't drawing any business. It was the free drinks and other party favors he was dishing out – not just to me, but to any quasi-star – that was driving his business down.

Between his bad management of the club, a coke habit to rival my own, and the shopping habits of both his mistress and his wife, Rick was just about broke and on the verge of closing his doors when I came up with project Cyber Hooker Dot Net. I bought him out for pennies on the dollar. I think he was a bit miffed about that, that I didn't give him what he thought of as a fair deal – especially after all the freebies he'd given me. But it was my deal or bankruptcy. I wasn't totally heartless; I did let him stay on as a pseudo-manager.

In addition to taking over his lease on the club, I optioned the lease on the empty office space behind the club. That wasn't too hard either, as the landlord didn't have many takers. Not many doctors or lawyers are looking to keep shop next to a strip club.

We knocked out the wall between the dressing room and the new office space and I had the whole place wired with something they call DSL cable. I'm not sure what the Hell that is, but that's why I hired one of those computer eggheads to tell me what we needed. Egghead also hauled in a few dozen computers, each one with some kind of special Internet video camera attached to it. And we divided the whole joint into cubicles – each furnished with its own bed.

What's amazing is I really didn't have to put up much cash out of pocket. Once you're a business, banks give you loans; leases are signed with nothing down; equipment is shipped on credit. Eventually the bills would come, of course, but in terms of cash up-front, I didn't even spend the $10K I withdrew from my savings.

For $69 bucks (I figured that was an appropriately sexually suggestive price tag) anyone could send the gift of a cyber hooker. Instead of Joe Homebody getting a knock at the door to find a skanky street ho waiting to be his 20 minute disease-carrying present, Joe Homebody got a 20 minute live session with a gorgeous young thing who just happened to be on the other end of a camera.

None of the girls in the club *had* to do the cyber hooker venture, they could still just dance if they wanted to. But those who wanted to turbo-charge their incomes could work in the back in between their dance sets.

My accountant said it was the stupidest thing he'd ever heard of. The thing about those Harvard, Cambridge, Yale types is that they don't realize most of America is stupid and likes stupid things.

My agent Steve thought the idea was brilliant and tried to convince me to let him buy in on it. By then he was used to the fact that my stupid ideas worked much better than the intelligent ones. I didn't let him buy in, but I did get him a cyber hooker for his birthday. I later found out his kid, little Stevie, intercepted the present. C'est la vie. Not like big Steve hadn't stolen his old man's Playboys when he was a kid. Same principle, different eras.

Cyber Hooker Dot Net Enterprises Ltd. turned out to be a success. Not just a little success. A **major** fucking success. There was so much money rolling in from Cyber Hooker Dot Net that we hardly felt a dent from Rick's continued bad management of the strip club. I think the thing is that the concept applied to more than one demographic. You learn about things like demographics when you've been pitching television series to studios. The studios want to know what demographic – what age, race, religion – of viewers the program is going to appeal to.

You have your typical Internet porn addicts who rack up credit card debts to look at naughty pictures on members-only sites. They were a natural target. But with something so obscurely titled as CyberHooker.Net there was also the curiosity user – the one looking for something new. There was the gift buyer market. You would never sign your friend up for a year-long membership at a porno web site, but it makes a great gag gift to send a one-time cyber hooker. The market wasn't just limited to gag gifts either – we found a lot of couples bought cyber hooker adventures to spice up their suburban, middle-aged love lives. Have the threesome you've always fantasized about, but with a virtual safety net.

What I think was my coup de gras was the murals. On the wall behind each bed, I had these pull-down backdrops. I got the idea from a Sears photography studio I took my cousin Rachel and her kids to for family pictures. At the touch of a button, the photographer would lower a backdrop of a fireplace, or one of a meadow, or one of a beach. The options were endless.

I put those in the cyber hooker cubicles. Not only did the viewer get a virtual date with a fantasy girl, he could pick the location for the rendezvous – Paris, Hawaii, on an airplane, even outer space.

Today the company is worth a couple billion. It's been bought and sold a few dozen times; I think some soft drink company owns it now. I sold out in my first year for $35 million. I was delusional; I thought my acting career actually mattered. When they offered me the $35 mil I didn't see dollar signs, I saw a way to finance my own film – to buy myself the kind of role I'm never going to get offered because my name isn't Tom Cruise or Brad Pitt.

A producer who knows what he's doing never uses his own money; he gets a studio to back him, or at the very least foreign money. I was a producer by default, not by trade. I didn't know the ins and outs, just that I wanted a shot to prove I was a real actor. So I used my own cash.

The film was called *Sacred Clone*. In it, the Catholic Church has grown tired of waiting for the Second Coming of Christ. Secretly in possession of the Shroud of Nazareth, they cross the line of creationism versus evolution and clone Jesus from the DNA on the Shroud. The plan is to raise the clone to be the new savior. The problem is that Baby Jesus II walks away when nobody's looking and ends up being raised on the streets, learning his morals from gangs and vagrants instead of from the Church. He ends up a murderer, seeking vengeance on the man who killed his drug addict girlfriend. As he is led to the electric chair, he tells the archbishop who cloned him, "I die for your sins." Of course, I played Jesus – well, the cloned Jesus.

If Universal had produced the film and Brad Pitt had starred, it would have been a classic. Not that Brad Pitt would have done the role any better, Universal just would have dumped a ton of cash into promoting the film because it was Brad Pitt. Whether a movie is a hit or not has nothing to do with how good it is, it's all about who backs it.

Even though *Titanic* was a schmaltzy tour de force of crapola, it won the Best Picture Oscar. Why? It won because it was produced by one major studio and distributed by a separate major studio.

Who votes on the Oscars? For the most part, the voters are employees of one form or another at major studios. So if you have all the employees at two of the biggest studios in the world strongly encouraged to cast their votes for a specific film, it's going to win. And the public is just stupid enough to buy into the hype.

Clone wasn't backed by a major studio. It was backed 100% by money I made from Cyber Hooker Dot Net. I'm not saying it was the greatest film ever made. If it was, nobody will ever know it. Nobody saw it. As producer de facto, I didn't know I had to keep money around to distribute the film. My accountant told me I had enough left to support my lifestyle *or* roll the dice on distributing the film, but not both. C'est la fucking vie.

I think the problem is I didn't want success bad enough. If I wanted success that bad, it would have been ok to gamble my final savings on distribution. Because if you want something that bad, you'll find a way to make it work. But I don't have that kind of fire in my gut.

I think there is something to be said for destiny, for the preordained. But sometimes I think those mapped-out lives also take wrong turns. For instance, I think some people are born to be stars – it's what they're meant to do. Other people are meant to spend their lives trying to become stars.

I was one of the people who was supposed to spend my life trying but always coming up short. That was my purpose in life. I was never supposed to become a star.

I don't know if the planets were out of alignment or what, but by some accident I went from wannabe to real life. And that's what ruined me.

Different things motivate different people. It was the trying to achieve that drove me. Once I'd done it, I had no motivation.

People meant to be stars don't strive for it, it just happens. Their life motivation is to stay stars. My life motivation was supposed to be to become a star. I was never preordained to become a star, so I never had the inherent drive to stay a star once it happened.

invincible youth, faded glory

Fame didn't corrupt me. I would have been a fuck up anyway. They say your emotional maturity is stunted the first time you have a drink or take a drug. I guess that explains why I have the emotional maturity of a child. I would have been a corrupt soul anyway. Fame just allowed me to do it in style.

I had my first drink when I was six. At least that's the first one I recall. When I was young my aunt was striving to be cool, her way of defying aging I guess. If young people thought she was cool then she wasn't "old." Whatever. If you ask me it actually makes an old person look not just old but old and desperate when they try so hard.

My old man felt guilty I didn't have a mother, so he was always shipping me off to my aunt's for visits, hoping she could be a female influence in my life. Being in the Midwest they had lots of barbecues. Barbecues mean kegs. Striving to be the cool aunt, Susan didn't hesitate to allow me a cup of beer. What harm could one little cup of beer do?

Beer is an acquired taste. All alcohol is. I think if they didn't tell you that you're not supposed to have it and that it's bad for you, then nobody would get started drinking. They'd have the first sip, realize it tastes like crap, and never drink enough to realize the pleasures of being drunk. But with the promise of euphoria so widely publicized, you stomach that first, second, and third glass. Eventually you learn to love the taste because you associate it with the after- effects.

I had my first cigarette when I was 9, also courtesy of my aunt. While Susan knowingly gave me my first drink, she was an unknowing donor to the beginning of my tobacco addiction. She left her cigarettes out all the time, would forget where she left the pack, and would open a new one. It was no hard task to steal a cigarette here and there, and as my addiction grew it was no hard task to steal a pack here and there.

The funny thing is that I always knew I would be a tobacco addict, even before I was one, even before I tried a single cigarette. At the age of 10 while watching the adults smoke during the intermission of *Oliver*, Jesse told me that he would never try cigarettes. All kids, it seems, make that claim at that age. Years later, egged on by peer pressure and Marlboro Man ads, they're three pack a dayers. But kids are innocent, they make innocent claims. Growing up is regrettably about losing your innocence, becoming bitter, learning to lie. Learning to lie is in its purest form when you lie to yourself, breaking the promises you made yourself as a child.

I never had a loss of innocence because I can't remember a time when I was innocent. When Jesse made the "I'm never going to smoke" claim, I didn't pipe in with the prerequisite "me too."

"I'll probably only smoke a pipe, it's not as bad for you," I replied. *Not as bad for you.* I already knew it was bad and I already knew I would smoke. My lying to myself was that I might be able to do it in some moderation – like use a pipe. The fact is, to this day I have never tried a pipe. Well, except for smoking pot. I went straight to the cancer sticks.

Pot is definitely not my drug of choice. I don't hate it, but I don't favor it. I do it, but I could do without it if I ever had to choose between my drugs of choice.

I get fucked up for two reasons. One is that my mind does not stop. When a normal person goes to bed, they go to sleep. When I go to bed, my mind keeps going. I'm writing six screenplays in my head simultaneously. I'm thinking about what I did today. I'm thinking about what I need to do tomorrow. I'm outlining a letter to the mother I never had asking why she didn't want me. I'm planning new business ventures that I'll never get around to launching. I forget more by 5 AM than most people think of in their lives. I'm an insomniac because I can't get my mind to stop. That is, unless I get fucked up enough to pass out.

Basically, any night that I want to sleep I have to drink. Alcohol is a depressant; it slows the mind. It's the best way I've found to shut my mind off. It never fully shuts off, but I get to a point where I can ignore the ideas long enough to fall asleep and have them become dreams.

Tennessee Williams used to write about that point – where you've had enough to drink that you just don't care. The demons, the brilliance, whatever you call it – it finally fades to a dull gray, white noise in the background. He called it "the click." He talked about it as if it was a light switch being turned off, something you heard or felt. For me it's not a click, not an instant that can be pinpointed. It's more something that can only be appreciated in retrospect. Eventually I'll realize I'm not overwhelmed with thoughts anymore. I couldn't tell you how long ago the gray had set in, just that it had.

The other reason I'll do drugs is the complete opposite: to enhance my enjoyment of life. That's why I love coke. It's a mood enhancer. If you're in a bad mood, it's not going to make you happy. It'll burn you further down. But if you are rocking, it will add to that adrenaline sky. That's when I like coke. Coke makes me at one with the electricity of life.

I was with Stuart Perotto the first time I tried coke. I guess we were like fifteen or sixteen or some shit like that. Stuart was the fuck up who didn't have to be a fuck up.

There are those kids in high school who have fucked-up hair and smoke cigarettes and cut class because that's what their role in life is supposed to be. They were born to be the white trash of the world. Their parents are white trash; their cousins are white trash. They have no choice but to be white trash.

Now, that's not saying every kid of white trash parents has to end up as white trash. There are some kids who turn out the exact opposite of their families. It's like they have a choice of how they want to learn. They can learn how to be white trash by emulating their parents, or they can learn how to avoid becoming white trash by doing the opposite of their parents.

Rich kids have the same choices. Rich kids can learn from their parents how to be successful, or they can rebel and not be like their parents and thus start a new generation of white trash. What's really odd is that so few kids in white trash families have the determination to rebel against white trashdom to strive to succeed, but such a high percentage of well-off kids decide to fuck up their lives to spite their parents. Parents whose biggest crime was giving their kids everything they ever asked for.

Stuart Perotto wasn't just a rich kid, he was a mega rich kid. His dad was the vice president of some Fortune 500 company. Maybe it was Fortune 100. Anyway, the kid came from money. "My dad makes more in an hour than your dad makes in a year," he once commented in that self pitying voice you only hear from really rich kids whose parents make too much money for them to ever be happy.

My friend Jesse was the polar opposite of Stuart. From the time he was 10 he was walking the five mile trek from the "only losers live there" apartments in town to the well-to-do areas to mow lawns to earn money. As soon as he was old enough to get a work permit he was bagging groceries at the supermarket in town. He still mowed lawns, it was just on the weekends so it wouldn't interfere with his other job.

Jesse was arguably the poorest kid in school. Yet, Jesse always wore suits to school. Sure he picked them up at Goodwill and the dry cleaning costs were more than what he paid for them, but they were suits – which is more than kids from ten times his income bracket were wearing. That's why he did it. Kids driving to school in their own BMWs that their parents bought for them, were wearing jeans with holes and unwashed t-shirts. Jesse, who had learned to live off one meal a day, wore suits.

In the ghetto kids sell drugs for the money. Rich kid Stuart Perotto got his start in the lucrative field of narcotics trafficking by fencing pot because he thought it was cool.

Stuart was a six-foot, four-inch Adonis who demolished opponents in every sport he competed in. But his five-foot, four-inch high school drop out older brother was the king of weed. By selling weed for his brother, Stuart figured he would not only gain the acceptance of his disapproving sibling, but his drug obsessed peers at school as well.

Stuart's biggest mistake wasn't selling drugs. Stuart's biggest mistake was trying the product he was distributing. Had he just dealt, Stuart would have had his brother's respect as a good drug dealing sibling, the respect of the other kids as a cool drug dealing jock, and plenty of extra money to celebrate the acceptance of family and friends.

However, as all good drug dealers do eventually, Stuart did start smoking up himself. Maybe pot isn't addictive physically speaking. But when it comes to psychological addictions, you can get addicted to goat cheese on your salad. Stuart needed to smoke pot. He didn't need to physically. He wasn't going to go into convulsions and puke up bile like a heroin addict. But that doesn't mean he didn't *think* he needed it.

The thing about pot is that it makes everything beautiful—until it wears off, that is. It's kind of like alcohol in that way. As long as you keep yourself in a perpetual state of being stoned, everything is beautiful. If you let yourself fall from the heavens of cannabis euphoria for the briefest of moments, the doldrums of depression don't just knock at your door, they've already knocked the door down and are feasting on your liver before you have even heard the doorbell ring.

I don't care if an addiction is psychological or physical, either way it means you're going to spend more money than you have to maintain that feeling. Stuart was no exception.

Stuart's day consisted of getting up, getting stoned, and getting ready for school. He'd crashed the Beamer his parents had given him one too many times and they'd stopped paying to get it fixed. So, after he'd missed the school bus, his mother would wake him up again and tell him to hurry and get dressed. After she left, he'd smoke up again. At school, having already missed half of first period, Stuart would roam the halls until he ran into someone who wanted to go smoke pot with him in the parking lot. Sometimes they'd nod off in the car, other times they'd head their separate ways to their second period classes. By lunch it was time to smoke up again – similar set of rules. Sometimes he'd make it to class, sometimes not. It didn't matter.

The biggest problem with Stuart's habit was that he wasn't just smoking up any potential profits he was making, he was going into some serious debt from his supplier. And, as lovably stupid as Stuart was, his five foot nothing brother and principal narcotics supplier was anything but forgiving. With his brother threatening to end Stuart's high school athletic career with two fractured kneecaps, Stuart moved from dealing pot to dealing coke because of the greater profit margin.

Stuart entered the cocaine business to get out from under the debt he incurred in the pot dealing business. Unfortunately the same need to know his product inspired Stuart when he switched from pot to coke. Within a few weeks of dealing it, Stuart went from never having touched the stuff to being a bona fide junkie.

I didn't see much of Stuart after that. It was a gradual but direct growth apart. He grew one of those little "if I had more testosterone this would be real facial hair" moustaches, and missed more and more classes until he went from being absent to being expected to be absent to being forgotten.

After he moved back to Denver and found himself married with children after drinking too much in Vegas, Jesse ran across Stuart. It's amazing from all perspectives that it was only a few years after high school.

Stuart was selling vacuum cleaners door to door and happened to ring Jesse's doorbell. Jesse said Stuart looked like a horse that had been ridden hard and put away wet. Any memory of youthful glow was gone. He looked like he could have been Jesse's father. Actually, the way Jesse put it was that "Age wise, Stuart looked like he could have been my father. But he had that lonely, depressed, burned out thing going on that made him look like he could never be anyone's father, just the forgotten uncle."

Stuart didn't recognize Jesse. He was performing his sales routine on automatic pilot. Jesse thought of reminding him they'd gone to school together, then thought better of it. It might embarrass Stuart to have someone who knew him in his invincible youth see him faded from glory. If he wasn't embarrassed to be recognized as he was, then Stuart wouldn't be above hitting up an old forgotten acquaintance for some money. Either way, Jesse thought it best to let the salesman move on by.

nailing neve campbell

My friend Jesse's marriage to his wife Patty was short lived, not surprising given that its foundation was questionable at best. I mean, what makes a marriage valid? Should remembering the ceremony be a requirement? If not, then is the validity established simply by a signed license being on file in some office of records somewhere? Or, does the signature on the license have to actually be yours?

Jesse went for a weekend getaway with a new girlfriend and woke up with a hangover, a barrage of credit card bills, a wife, and two kids. Sounds more like something that I'd have done.

Patty, the marital partner in question, assured Jesse that the wedding he didn't recall had been a charade. In an inebriated state they'd bought the license and ring, but hadn't sought out any justice of the peace to legitimize the union. It was, she explained simply an act so she could claim to the government to have moved out of her parents' home and thus qualify for increased welfare money. Patty was the queen of milking the system — when she wasn't busy milking the pockets of her suitors.

If I come across a bit harsh and jaded about Patty, it's because I am. It's hard to feel sorry for someone who manufactures reasons to be the victim without regard to who might become the villain in the process.

Anyway, it was a joke between them. One of those jokes that has a little more than a hint of truth to it. That kind of tension that used to make *Moonlighting* an enjoyable show to watch. She'd jokingly refer to him as her husband, but there was always some hint of truth to it. Sometimes it would be more truth than jest, other times it was the jest that was paramount. But a visit from the postman changed all that a few months after the forgotten Vegas extravaganza.

One day, their marriage certificate arrived in the mail. Patty had said they'd bought the license but hadn't formalized the nuptials. I don't care how immoral Vegas might be, even its civil servants don't issue marriage certificates that haven't been formally and duly filed, processed, signed, sealed, and delivered by one of the area's numerous 24 hour justices of the peace.

Ironically, Patty didn't deny what now appeared to have happened. She didn't offer any explanation or excuse. "We'll go out to dinner and I'll explain everything," she cooed as Jesse set out on his daily errands of dropping his inherited children off at day care and going to work. Several times throughout the day, he called the woman who was apparently not his girlfriend but actually was his wife, but he just kept getting voicemail.

When Jesse showed up that evening for his scheduled dinner date and fact finding mission, all his things were packed up in bags on Patty's front porch. "It's not working out," she explained through the locked front screen door before deadbolting herself inside. Two days later Jesse was served with divorce papers, demanding half of his savings and property as well as child support for children who had grown accustomed to his paternal influence despite not being related by means of genetics or adoption.

Poor Jesse, not only had she just bent him over and screwed him like an Arkansas field hand befriends a pig, he didn't even get it. His ass had been raped and was lying bloody and exposed and he had no idea. He still loved her. He still loved the kids. He didn't fight the baseless demands for child support. He continued to call Patty, to beg her to work things out with him.

His advances and dedication didn't faze Patty. If anything, they angered her. She didn't want to be loved, couldn't accept being loved. She wanted Mike back because he had left her. Since she had left Jesse, she would never want him back. There was no need.

Jesse was calling me nightly. Sometimes he just needed someone to talk to because the alternative was to drink. Other times he'd call because he hadn't previously sought out an alternative to drink and thus was drunk-dialing to dispel the woes that had inspired him to drink in the first place.

I did my best with the calls. Let's face it, I'm no shrink. And I've never had a real relationship to speak of, so I couldn't offer much advice from experience. But I tried to listen as much as I could. Night after night, he'd call with story after story of how he was determined to get her back, but she was pretending to be out of town. Her mother was telling him to leave them alone and accept that she was gone, that she'd moved to California. But he wasn't going to buy it. He was going to hire a detective. He was going to convince her to come back.

I really did try to be understanding. I was at the peak of my fame. I was shooting the series during the days, leaving the house at 5 A.M. to get to the lot for makeup. I had at my fingertips an all-you-can-eat pass to the smorgasbord of groupies that celebrity provides, and yet I was staying home night after night to console Jesse when his inevitable call would come. But over time, I just couldn't any more.

One evening I gave myself the night off from phone duty to go try at least one of the 31 flesh flavors offered up by stardom. Even then, I thought if I worked fast enough maybe I wouldn't miss being there for Jesse.

I ended up with a dead ringer for Neve Campbell. I swear, Neve herself didn't look as much like Neve Campbell as this chick did. I'd picked her up at Skybar, or rather she'd picked me up. She was a chick who knew what she wanted and she knew she wanted me. Who was I to object? I'd always had a hard-on for Neve, so why not take advantage of the next best thing, fantasy fulfillment presenting itself to me?

She screwed like she was on a mission. It was that raw unbridled sex that makes you want to climax with every fiber in your body, but also makes you not want to peak at all because you don't want it to ever end. There was no emotion, no love, just sex. The room stank of sex. It was raw. Pure and simple. No holds barred. It was pounding from behind, slapping her ass, making her scream kind of raw. It was bite marks on bite marks kind of raw. It was fluids you didn't even know existed from places and into places you didn't think possible. It was licking up every drop of essence and begging for more, should be doing it for money it's that good kind of raw.

During our rapture, Jesse did call – as he did every night, several times a night. For once, I ignored the call. It played in the background. But I was otherwise occupied.

The finish was amazing, her bent down between my legs. I was panting and aching in the afterglow. She smiled a coy vixen look of delight, licking her lips for show and tell.

"There's towels down the hall," I offered from my prone position on the couch in the living room. Plain and simple, I couldn't have moved to play host had I desired to or had her persona dictated it. With a smile she strode down the hall, her perfect ass disappearing from view. Then came her voice from down the hall, talking into the phone. She was not speaking to me, but all the same speaking loud enough for my benefit.

"Hi Jesse, it's Patty. You remember how you said if I was ever in LA, I should look up your friend the movie star? You'll never guess whose brains I just fucked out of his skull."

I kind of went numb, only vaguely hearing the door shut as Patty let herself out of my home.

I guess if you want to look at the silver lining, Jesse finally did give up on getting Patty back. That's when Jesse took his vow of celibacy. It was years before he would meet Andrea, and he never

142

broke that moral decision – at least not until after Andrea left him at the figurative altar.

We never talked about the night of Patty's phone call, Jesse and I. If he didn't ask if it was true, I didn't have to answer. Sometimes it's better to not know the truth, to do what is necessary to hold on to the chance of an alternative reality. As long as we didn't talk about it, he could hold on to the chance that her call hadn't been from my house. Or, even if it was, the chance that her purpose for being there wasn't as she described.

We pretended it didn't affect our friendship. He'd still come to visit sometimes. We'd still talk on the phone. I even started visiting him in Denver.

In time the awkwardness faded, and with it at least some of the pain. Not all of it though. A piece of that night was always there, a painful silence between us.

I didn't know it was Patty. She played me the same way she'd played Jesse. But knowing that doesn't give me back the life-long trust I shared with my best friend. If she had just taken his money, she would have been a bitch. But she did more than that; far more than that. She took his dignity. And for what?

romeo and gilligan

Although we did it for different reasons, like Jesse I also retired from acting at one point. Jesse gave up the fight because he knew that he'd never win, that forces behind the curtain would make sure the puppet would never dance on the main stage. I think, also, the death of his mother made him lose hope. She believed in him. She believed he could overcome the insurmountable odds stacked against him. As long as she believed in him, he did too. That belief died with her.

I, on the other hand, retired from acting because I thought I was in love.

I am the bastard child of a borderline hermit, full-blown hypochondriac and a woman he met in bar and never saw again after I was born. My best friend was the bastard child of an alcoholic mother and a father who not only didn't acknowledge him but did everything in his power to deny his existence. Having never really witnessed a healthy relationship growing up, I had no point of comparison to know what love was.

Taking a retrospective look at life, I realize now that the reason I became a performer was that I didn't get the kind of affection I needed growing up. My father was a good man, but he wasn't very open with his emotions. He wasn't the type to give a hug for no reason. Hell, he wasn't the type to give a hug even when it was apparent someone needed one. He was just too insecure.

My dad was my family. I didn't have a mother around or sisters or brothers. Outside of two summers with my aunt and my

144

cousin Rachel, it was just me and my nonaffectionate father. That might be ok for some people, but I'm just a touchy-feely person by nature. I have always needed praise, needed to be touched, needed to be loved.

The only thing I ever found that was close to acceptance, much less affection, was on stage – the applause from the audience. That's why I made it my career – because I didn't know any better but to think that was the only kind of gratification there is in life.

I met Barbie when I was 22. Her name was actually Jan, but I called her Barbie. The joke was that she thought I called her Barbie because she collected Barbie dolls. You can probably figure out the real reason – more silicone than Pamela Anderson and less upstairs than a one story house. But she was sweet. And, most of all, she loved me.

My series had been off the air about a year, *Romeo Now* had just flopped at the box office, and I hadn't had any serious offers since wrapping up a James Dean television miniseries. I still had some level of fame, though. It was when I still had my "big time" agent, before my career bottomed out and Steve picked me out of the dumpster and reinvented my career via the wonderful world of cable TV movies of the week and straight-to-video features.

At the time, my "big time" agent kept reassuring me another movie deal was right around the corner, and to keep busy she convinced me to do a theatrical tour. Tell me that doesn't mean your career is dying.

Grease was touring at the time. Following in the tradition of the Broadway revival, they were rotating in as many celebrities as possible – pop singers, Olympic athletes, professional wrestlers, and falling stars like me. Donny Most of *Happy Days*, Peter Scolari of *Bosom Buddies*, Jeff Conaway who played Kinickie in the film version of *Grease*, and Davy Jones of *The Monkees* all took their turn in the freak show revival. So, I signed on to play Danny Zuko.

My first stop was going to be Chicago and we were scheduled for at least 2 months. I had my cat Romeo with me back then. That was one of the conditions in my contract, they paid to have my cat travel with me on the tour. I wasn't a big enough star any more to make any real demands like only red M&M's in my dressing room, so I settled for cat accommodations.

I have "best friends" who are people, but Romeo truly is my best friend in the whole world. I honestly believe that pets are much better doctors than doctors are. Whenever I'm sick Romeo will curl up on my chest and stay with me until I feel better. I think I'll know I've found "the one" when I find a girl who curls up with me when I'm sick. I'm not looking for someone to get me soup or wait on me, I just want someone who will curl up with me and wait out the storm.

I got Romeo when I was campaigning for the title role in the *James Dean* miniseries. The director was a tad quirky – imagine that in Hollywood. One of her quirks was that she volunteered at an animal shelter – when you're rich and powerful, you can afford to throw your time around on noble causes.

My agent sent me to the animal shelter to kiss up to the director. I figured taking a cat home was a small price to pay for a primo role – even if it was only a movie of the week. I was going to take Mindy home. She was an older cat with a weepy eye. I figured nobody else would want her, so why take a pretty kitten out of the hands of some kid? But there was one cat, about a year old, that would meow whenever I got near his cage. He wouldn't meow for anyone else. The director noticed and insisted I hold him. He hugged me like a baby. I had to take him; he'd claimed me as his.

On the ride home I talked to the little meow about his name. He was one of the few cats there that had never been named. At first I suggested Sabas in honor of Arvydas Sabonis, the legendary Soviet basketball player. But it just didn't seem to fit: 7 foot 3 inch, 300-pound mountain of a man/little pretty boy cat. Next I suggested Judas. I really love the play *Jesus Christ Superstar* and always thought Judas got a bad rap for just doing what Christ set him up to do. But I figured that name might give the cat a complex. Not to mention, having a cat named Judas just might give the wrong impression to my potential dates.

Next on the list was Valentino. I love that name. If I ever have a kid I want to name it Valentino or Valentina (depending on if it's a boy or a girl). But I wouldn't want the kid to end up with a complex thinking it had been named after the cat. So, that one was out too.

Stuck on that lover boy theme, I suggested Romeo. When I said it, my little cat meowed. It was the first time he'd "talked" since we got in the car. I took that as a vote of approval.

I got the *James Dean* role and the director insisted that I bring Romeo on location for the shoot. Romeo's traveled with me ever since.

Barbie loved Romeo. Everyone loves Romeo. He's just the sweetest, smartest little guy in the world. He's a Hell of a lot smarter than me. But, Barbie also tended to go on about how she had always wanted a dog and her parents wouldn't let her have one in their house. Yeah, she was 24 and still lived with her parents.

I was love struck. After hearing how much she wanted a dog about 20 thousand times I agreed she could get a dog and I'd take care of it. Enter Juliet.

The dog Barbie showed up with one Saturday afternoon is probably the dumbest dog in history. Whereas Romeo is loveable because he's smart, this dog is lovable because she is just so gangly, awkward, and lacking of a brain.

Jesse came to visit me for a few weeks to the see the show and meet Barbie. Jesse took to calling the dog "one third." The joke was that Barbie, the dog, and Barbie's mother shared a brain – one third each. I loved Barbie, but she wasn't real bright, and neither was her mother. Jesse elaborated the story along those lines. The dog, he said, was the smartest third.

Barbie thought it would be cute to call the puppy Juliet. That way I'd have "Romeo and Juliet." I guess it never occurred to her that this dog was not a Juliet. A Juliet would be beautiful and graceful. When I moved out of my penthouse apartment and into a two-story townhouse, Juliet didn't know she was in a different place. She just went around trying to figure out where the stairs came from.

For all her stupidity, Juliet was lovable as all get out. She'd follow me around on my heels all the time, getting under foot. I took to calling her my "little buddy." Since that's what the Skipper called Gilligan on *Gilligan's Island*, it was only natural that she came to be called Gilligan. It just seemed to fit.

Barbie was studying to be a beautician when I met her. Chances are she is probably still studying to be a beautician. When we met she'd been in beauty school for three years. From what I understand, it's not normally supposed to take that long.

What she lacked in intelligence, Barbie made up for in determination. Even if it was going to take the rest of her life – which it might – she was determined to one day participate in the graduation ceremonies of D'Monroe Beauty College. Nobody had the heart to tell her that beauty schools don't typically have graduation ceremonies.

The producers of *Grease* were very committed to promoting the show. They were brilliant at concocting the quirky types of off-beat marketing events that newspapers eat up – entering our Greased Lightning car from the show in races at the local drag strip, or offering half-price tickets to people who dress up as their favorite character.

Grease features the memorable comic song "Beauty School Drop Out." Frankie Avalon immortalized the song in the 1978 film as the Teen Angel. To capitalize on the fame of the song and create yet another can't-miss marketing event, our producers had a special Beauty School Night. Anyone currently in classes at D'Monroe (thus, not a beauty school drop out) received a free ticket and a chance to pose for pictures with the cast after the show. It didn't hurt that it created a fantastic photo opportunity for all the TV stations and newspapers in town.

Barbie had been one of the guests that night. There was just something so innocently charming about the way she really liked *Romeo Now*. She wasn't saying it to impress me. She honestly thought it was good, the same way she honestly didn't understand *The Brady Bunch* was in reruns.

We didn't jump into a relationship right away. First we dated casually – but the fact was, neither one of us was seeing anyone else, nor did we want to. She would get all nervous and ask these funny little questions – like after we'd been dating for a while she asked, "So are we just dating, or are we *dating*?"

A few weeks later she took the next nervous step, "So, since we're only seeing each other does that mean I can call you my boyfriend?" It was almost like she'd never dated before. But it was cute. There was no pressure about it; it was just stating what we both wanted.

What really attracted me to her – what made it go from a connection to an attraction – was the sincerity of her affection. She'd give me little gifts. Nothing extravagant, but things that showed she was thinking of me. One time she crocheted me a heart. Another time she bought me little superhero action figures – just because she passed them in a store and thought of me.

She was always telling me in writing that she loved me, and I could tell by her actions that it wasn't just words. The funny thing was she would never say those words, only write them. I liked that, though – no pressure. I was beginning to fall in love with her too, and I didn't want to ruin it by either one of us rushing it. It was natural and it felt good.

It finally happened at a Rick Springfield concert, of all places. After dropping off the face of the entertainment world for a decade, Rick was cashing in on the whole nostalgia thing with a new tour. He'd play small clubs so they'd always sell out; either that or state fairs where admission is free but the band gets a cut of the bar receipts, which are always brisk.

But hey, I'm not knocking him. You take the cash where you can. And I hope I look that good when I'm 50. Then again, who am I kidding? The chances of me reaching 50 are about on par with the chances of my getting cast in a biographical movie about the Harlem Globetrotters.

Barbie and I were at the concert and I'd had enough to drink that although I was still coherent, the laws of logic no longer applied. I asked if she wanted to go backstage. Rather awed, she said yes, then asked how.

Good question. But when the laws of logic have ceased to apply, "how" doesn't require specifics, planning, or much more than an ability to surf the tides of whatever happens-happens.

I approached the guard at the rear gate. "I'm on the list, plus one." I announced, acting nonchalant and highbrow aloof. Exhibiting the superior intellect that had landed him this minimum wage position, official orange rain slicker, and heavy-duty flashlight he replied "huh?"

I explained who I was, which should have amounted to instant access to a small show like this. I may not have been at the peak of celebrity anymore, but I hadn't fallen out of the gossip pages just yet. And in Chicago, my name and face were everywhere advertising *Grease*. Apparently my friend at the gate wasn't too up on gossip pages or theatre. "Huh?" he said again.

On a whim I flashed my union card. "I'm with the union," I said.

I don't remember if it was an AFTRA card or a SAG card, but neither one has anything to do with concerts. The American Federation of Television and Radio Artists covers television and radio, the Screen Actors Guild covers film. My friend at the gate seemed pretty impressed though, because he let us right in with two all-access passes.

Anyway, it was at that concert that Barbie told me she loved me. Girls have always told me they loved me. I don't mean that egotistically. Actually I mean it rather cynically. They always said it and I never believed it because there was nothing to believe. They loved an image. They didn't love me, they wanted me – that would be a more accurate description.

When Barbie told me she loved me, though, she meant it. She actually believed it. So for the first time, I believed it. And I loved her back. At least I convinced myself that I loved her back, because for the first time in my life someone really did love me and wasn't just wanting me.

That night was the turning point with Barbie. Maybe it was because the security guard didn't know who I was. Maybe because he thought I was a "normal" person and not a star, I was able to see myself as a normal person capable of a normal life like a wife and kids and a house in the suburbs.

Oh sure, celebrities have wives and kids, but usually it's a wife arranged by an agent to disprove the tabloid stories of homosexuality. The agent matches the star up with some unknown actress they also represent, and in exchange for going through the motions of marriage the girl gets instant celebrity. Usually there's also a clause for a guaranteed child and an option for a second – the same way studios contract actors for a guaranteed sequel and option for a third.

That night with Barbie, though, I was picturing a real marriage, real kids, and a real house in a real suburb – not a sterile mansion in a gated community where you don't know your neighbors — your security chief knows their security chief.

Grease was just a few weeks away from closing up shop in Chicago and trucking on down the road to Philadelphia, then Boston, and then D.C.

Barbie had lived in the same neighborhood all her life, had hung out with the same people all her life. In fact, I was the first guy she'd ever dated who wasn't from the neighborhood. So the concept of a world outside that neighborhood didn't really compute in her brain. It was the big scary unknown. Thus, the idea of hitting the road with me when *Grease* left Chicago wasn't something she was ready to do.

So, when *Grease* pulled up stakes and rolled out of Chicago, it was without me. I figured it was worth it to stay. So I did. I dropped out of the tour and "retired" from acting – at least for a few weeks.

sweet jimmy blues

My first job after "retiring" from acting to live a normal life with Barbie was in the literary field. Actually, to be technical, I was a cashier in an adult bookstore. Which I guess isn't even the literary field in the most general term, as that adult bookstores don't sell adult books – they sell videos and magazines. No books. Believe me, I know.

Let's face it, when you've never had a "real" job in your whole life, you don't get too many people lining up to hire you. Dana Plato after *Different Strokes*? Cashier at a dry cleaners. Danny Bonaduce after the *Partridge Family*? Maitre d' in a Chinese restaurant.

I mean, what do you put on your resume: former star? The fact is, I wasn't even qualified to work in the porno shop if you consider a 16-year-old drive through attendant from McDonalds had more experience than me. I think I only got the job because three of my references were in rehab clinics. Fat Ed, the owner but not proprietor (he spent all his time at his other business, a tattoo parlor), thought that was funny so he hired me.

The front of the shop is where I worked, behind the counter, ringing up the purchases. Up front there were two rows of general skin magazines ranging from innocent stuff like Playboy to fetish stuff like *Big Boob Hotties* and *Over 40* (and they weren't talking about size). The third aisle had the hardcore show-it-all mags and the real whacked out stuff – pregnant girls having sex, amputees having sex, close ups of piercings on body parts that just shouldn't be pierced. Across from the super smut aisle were the gay magazines. Don't ask me what was in them -- after the piercing magazine my casual curiosity about how the other half lives went away.

Winding around the store were the videos – floor to ceiling. They weren't alphabetical; the only kind of person who would come in looking for a specific title wouldn't be coming in anyway. They weren't even arranged by category. It was just a matter of: when there was a spot vacant on the wall, you put up a new video. *Barely Legal Teens 4* could be next to *Naughty Grannies* and it wouldn't matter. People tend to just look at the boxes until they're so worked up they have to leave, at which point they just grab whatever the closest movie is.

In the back was "The Cat Box." That was Fat Ed's attempt at being a literary highbrow – use two synonyms for pussy as the name of the stage where the girls do their sex show. I guess it didn't occur to him that a cat box also happens to be where cats shit.

My duties were pretty simple: ring up purchases and put new magazines and videos on the shelf when a space opened up. It was all pretty simple, in theory. But I'd never worked a cash register in my life, and Fat Ed's training regime involved handing me the keys to the store and a hand-scrawled description of my duties on a Burger King napkin. When I asked when my shift was over he told me "when someone else shows up."

So I was pretty much left to guess at prices and more so how to ring them up. It was pretty quick that I developed a system. Most customers are regulars, maybe not to the same porno store over and over, but to porno stores in general. So, they know the ballpark of how much things cost. Thus they always hand over more than enough money before you ask for it. On top of that, they're always in a rush to scoot out the door – either because they're embarrassed to be there or because they can't wait to get their torrid little treasure home. Either way, they never count their change. What are they going to do if it's wrong anyway? Make a scene? Yeah, right.

I figured the guy was always handing me just a little bit over the amount of his purchase. So I'd always give $1.43 in change. It was an odd number, so it seemed like it might be genuine. It included a bill, so it didn't have the glaring distinction of just being coins. And, by including a nickel, a dime, a quarter, and three pennies it seemed like a justifiable handful. The customers never complained and neither did Fat Ed, so I never bothered to learn the cash register.

Stocking the shelves wasn't too big a deal. Outside of knowing where the gay stuff went versus the straight stuff, and being able to tell a video from a magazine, there wasn't much to it. Besides, if I didn't get around to it, Fat Ed was never there so he wouldn't know if it was me stocking the shelves or someone else.

My favorite customer at the porno store was Sweet Jimmy Blues. Sweet Jimmy had to be in his late sixties, at least. He always came in a rumpled suit of some sort, usually black. Usually with a beaten old fedora too. He looked like the quintessential road traveled blues man. That's why I named him Sweet Jimmy Blues. I don't know if he ever played the blues in his life or if he was a legendary star on the sly, but to me he was Sweet Jimmy Blues. Hell, I should have become his manager and put him on tour. I could have got him bookings just for looking like a blues man.

Sweet Jimmy was a soft-spoken Negro gent. I say Negro on purpose, he thought the term "African-American" was politically-correct bullshit. He was Negro and proud of it.

Sweet Jimmy Blues had that gravel scarred voice you can only get from drinking cheap bourbon and smoking filterless cigarettes. He didn't speak much, but was always polite and he always had a faint twinkle in his eye. He'd been around when blacks had to use separate washrooms and ride in the back of the bus; he didn't feel any shame for walking in a store of any kind. He didn't hide his eyes like a lot of the hot shot Brooks Brothers types. He was as matter of fact as if he was going in a coffee shop to get a bite to eat.

Jimmy never bought magazines or videos. He liked the real thing. He came in just for the Cat Box show.

The girls who worked the Cat Box worked for tips. So there wasn't really a set schedule. If a girl showed up, she could go on. If more than one showed up, they could go work it together. Or, if they didn't want to share, it was first come, first served. If no girls showed up, then there was no show.

Sweet Jimmy Blues and I had our own way of speaking. He'd amble in and nod hello. I'd nod back. He'd nod towards the back room. "Chick?" he'd ask, keeping words to a minimum. And depending on if anyone was working or not, I'd answer "Chick" in the affirmative or "No chick" in the negative. Either way he'd nod his thanks and either proceed to the back room if there was a show, or amble back out the door if the Cat Box was empty. That was Sweet Jimmy Blues.

I wasn't allowed to get too friendly with any of the girls who worked the cat room. Not because of any rules of Fat Ed, he didn't care if the staff boinked each other as long as it wasn't on his time. It was a self-imposed rule since I was trying to have a relationship with Barbie.

But I'm a friendly guy, and just because I wasn't screwing the girls didn't mean I couldn't chat with them. They fell into three categories – the regulars, the transients, and the wannabes. The regulars were girls who had resigned themselves to the fact that, like it or not, this was their line of work, and Fat Ed's Cat Box was where they did it. They were usually a few years past their prime, not fooling themselves that they could cut it in actual strip bars anymore. Most had a high school education, maybe some community college. They weren't stupid, but they weren't educated enough to get a job as anything but a waitress or secretary, and even working for tips in a nasty hole like Fat Ed's paid better than that.

The transients were girls between jobs. Maybe they were club dancers who'd refused to get friendly with the owner anymore so they were given the boot, and at Fat Ed's there wasn't much of a waiting list. It paid their rent and fed their coke habit while they looked for a new club or finally decided blowing the owner was worth the tips at the hot spot strip clubs.

The wannabes were the girls who just couldn't accept that they weren't strip club material. Maybe they used to be and their beauty had started to fade – partying can age a girl quick, and a beauty at a dance club has a lot of chances to party. Some never had the beauty to be a real stripper and just didn't realize it. A rare few had the looks, but just lacked the charisma to really sell it.

Whatever the case, the wannabes would work for a while, all the time talking about how they were going to make it out of this place. Then, they'd leave for a while. But eventually they'd come back – either with glorified tales of their vast successes that never seemed to add up to why they're back at Fat Ed's, or just refusing to talk about the humiliation they faced out in the real world.

Darla was the queen bee of Fat Ed's. In the pecking order for back room dancers at porno shops, and believe me there is one, Darla was at the top of the food chain. She must have been about 35. You never ask these girls about their age. It wouldn't matter if you did, if they're underage they'll say they're 18, if they're in their 20s then they're always 20. If they're on the wrong side of 30, then they're 27. Nobody is over 27.

Darla probably wouldn't have lied about her age though, if I'd bothered to ask. She had that Susan Sarandon quality of confidence in her sexuality. That confidence made her the best.

She'd done some porno work when she was younger. None of that high-gloss, Glamour Shots box cover stuff you see today. She wasn't a featured girl – the ones with names like Pamela Peeks or Mercedes Luscious. She was a background player – the nameless girl who bats cleanup because the big name starlet on the box cover has some goofy idea that it's okay to be in a pornographic movies as long as she doesn't finish anything she starts.

Darla was never bitter about her porno past. She didn't mind talking about intimate encounters with produce, candles, and kitchen utensils. She also didn't hold any false belief that she had been any more than a background player. She told her stories in the same way anyone else reflects on amusing anecdotes from their past jobs. Hers just happened to involve KY Jelly.

a spotlight built for one

Shortly after I dropped out of the *Grease* tour to stay in Chicago with Barbie, my agent called with another stage show in the city. My brief retirement had taught me pretty quick that I really wasn't cut out for real work. So I was ecstatic when my agent called with a gig.

Granted, I'd have much rather she had been calling with a series in a less cheese-obsessed, blue-collar city. But, as long as I was in Chicago, working in a hit play was better than nothing, and certainly better than Fat Ed's Porno Shop and Cat Box Show.

Tony n' Tina's Wedding had been running in Chicago for something like nine years straight. I'm guessing at the number, but it can't be far off. The show was far and away the city's number one box office comedy. Described as "environmental theatre," the concept is that the audience is actually part of the action. It's not actors up on a stage putting on a little play; the audience members are actually the guests at an Italian wedding in a real chapel, followed by a reception in a neighboring banquet hall.

Anyone who's ever been to an Italian wedding (which basically includes the entire population of Chicago, thus the play's popularity there) knows it can be a bizarre and humorous explosion of drunken emotion, sexual impropriety, fistfights, macho bravado, patriarchal speeches, and off key singing. Now, that's a real Italian wedding. *Tony n' Tina's* takes all those stereotypes and pushes the envelope of humor with *Saturday Night Live* style parody.

The show had originally started in New York, Off-Broadway. New York being another city whose population has unanimously been exposed to Italian weddings, the show was a natural hit and is still running to this day. Hell, it will probably keep running as long as the producers want to keep making money – there will always be an audience for it.

Over time, the producers began licensing the rights to investors to open productions in other cities. Philadelphia was a success. Again, it's a city that is a hotbed of Italian culture. Los Angeles, on the other hand, was a flop. If the city doesn't have a "Little Italy" neighborhood, then it's not a *Tony n' Tina's* market.

Joey and Anthony Tomaska picked up the rights for Chicago. Anthony, the older of the brothers, is a no-nonsense business whiz who had previously dabbled in producing films. His biggest credit was a film called *Shaking the Tree* starring a then-unknown Courtney Cox. It didn't do well when it was made, but repackaged after Courtney hit it big on *Friends*, the film probably bankrolled the Tomaska brother's future projects.

Younger brother Joey was an actor who'd done a few small guest spots on TV. After a nose job and an exercise program he had the movie star looks to catch the eye of pre-Arquette Cox.

As far as *Tony n' Tina's* went, Anthony produced and Joey starred. The show was a smash hit. And, being so heavily improvised based upon audience interaction, the show was never the same twice. That's what keeps audiences coming back over and over.

At the time I was in Chicago, the Tomaskas were looking to expand their *Tony n' Tina's* empire. Most of the other prime U.S. markets were already licensed to other producers. So, Anthony set his sights east, across the Atlantic, and secured the rights for a London production.

It was decided that in order to get the London production off on the right foot, Joey would cross the ocean and headline the cast there. This, of course, would leave the Chicago production without its star.

Ever the businessman, Anthony saw this as an opportunity to breath new life into his Chicago franchise – attract a new audience and give the old faithful something brand new to come back for. Anthony wanted to bring in a name star who would draw an audience but wouldn't bankrupt his budget. Guess who fit the bill?

I was a nationally known TV star. I was still considered a hunk by the gossip magazines. And I'm Italian. Best of all, I was in Chicago, bored off my ass, and available to work at a bargain rate just for something to do.

No sooner had the billboards with my picture on them advertising *Grease* gone down, billboards of me advertising *Tony n' Tina's Wedding* went up. As an added bonus, since I was the first big name guest star in the history of any of the U.S. *Tony n' Tina's* productions, I was featured on all those fluffy entertainment daily shows across the country. Well, all of them except *Entertainment Tonight*. I don't know why they've never liked me. Maybe Mary Hart is jealous of my legs.

The game plan was for me to come in and watch the show for about a week and then step into the role of Tony, the groom. Performing six days a week, there really wasn't time to have a full cast rehearsal in order to plug me into the mix. Besides, since most of the show is improvised, without an audience it'd be kind of hard to rehearse anyway.

Plans do have a tendency to change, especially in the "show must go on" entertainment biz. I watched my first show on a Thursday. When I got to the theatre on Friday to watch my second show, I was quickly outfitted with a groom's tuxedo. Joey had been called to London that afternoon. With no rehearsal and having only seen the show once, I was starting that night.

All in all, it didn't go bad at all. Not realizing I'd be performing, I'd had a few drinks before heading to the theatre. Upon hearing I was going on with no preparation, I had a few more drinks. My engine was running on high octane when I hit my opening entrance, and I drove that racecar at daredevil speed, flirting with danger all night. The audience and the cast loved it. Based on that success, I never performed that role without a full tank of gas.

For the next year, I was THE man, in THE show, in the city. On the national level I was a decent sized fish. But in the small pond of Chicago, I was a whale. I couldn't pay for a cab ride or for dinner at a restaurant, everything was on the house for Mr. Big Time. That's something I've never understood – why give your product for free to big cheese actors and business tycoons who have more than enough money to be overcharged? Wouldn't it make more sense to give the freebies to people who could actually use a handout?

It wasn't just free food I was getting. I couldn't walk down the street without being stopped for autographs and pictures. Every morning show in town, albeit radio or TV, wanted to interview me. The local FOX morning program even had a daily update on where I'd been sighted the day before.

Barbie was someone who liked attention; liked it a lot. By being around me, some of my spotlight naturally cast light on her as well. When crowds would gather to ask for my autograph, she was by my side in the center of the crowd. Sometimes fans would ask her if she was famous too. Or they would assume she was and just ask for her autograph as well.

For someone who longs for attention and has never experienced it on that grand a scale, it must be an amazing experience. The problem is, once you get used to that kind of attention and the initial euphoria wears off, you realize that you're not the center of attention at all. In fact, you're less noticed then ever because you're in the shadow of someone people find more interesting than you. Someone who lives for attention doesn't like being in shadows, watching someone else get all the glory. That's what I'm guessing was going on for Barbie. Of course that's a retrospective guess. At the time, I had no idea. All I knew was that something was changing.

Barbie was never going to be happy sharing my spotlight. She wanted the attention on her. She would rather be the most interesting person in a room of three than a supporting player on the world's stage.

There was no blow up fight or tear-drenched goodbye. Gradually we were seeing less of each other. Going out with her friends alone where she could be the main focus as the girlfriend of the famous actor became more appealing to her than doing things with the famous actor. Looking back I realize that in the last two months of our dating she backed out of every single date except for things that we had nonrefundable tickets for.

One day my phone rang, it was Steve – an upstart agent wondering if I was seeking new representation. My big time agent had dropped me shortly after I started doing *Tony n' Tina's Wedding*. She said she couldn't bother herself with a theatre actor.

Steve said he had a project lined up for me if I was interested – a movie of the week. I packed my bags and left that day – with Romeo and Gilligan, of course.

working stiff

The last time I worked, truly worked, it was on a real film. Not some crummy non-union, shot in a day piece of crap. Not some hokey made-for-TV movie. Not some let's see what has-been we can find theatre tour. This was a real movie, with real stars.

The premier was in April. I know I'm no Hamlet. I wasn't there to play Hamlet. I was a supporting character, and that was fine. It was a chance to work again – not to just earn money, a chance to work.

At the premier reporters asked me if this was my comeback. I'm not even thirty and I've fallen so far they're talking about a supporting role as a comeback. It must have been how John Travolta felt with *Pulp Fiction*.

Sitting there watching the film with everyone else, I found out they'd cut some of my scenes. Actually, all in all, my role was reduced to my body double's hand ringing the doorbell, and me saying "Hi. Is Susan home?" That was it.

I was supposed to start work on a movie when I found Jesse's body. We were both supposed to start work on the movie.

Jesse had finally thrown in the towel and decided to come out of retirement and do the one thing he'd always vowed he'd never do: exploit his famous lineage. He'd always avoided that trap because he knew it would make him a joke – not just as an actor, but as a person. He didn't care anymore.

Some might argue he was doing it to get even with the famous family that had destroyed his chances for a legitimate career. That's what I thought when he asked me to do the project with him. In retrospect, though, I don't think it had anything to do with how he thought it might hurt his relatives. I think who he wanted to hurt was himself.

We were going to shoot the film in the deserts of New Mexico. Rather than just fly in, Jesse and I had decided to make a road trip of it and see what kind of trouble we could get into on the way there.

I flew into Denver in the morning, rented a Blazer, and swung by to pick up Jess at his house. We'd leave from there. At least that was the plan.

They recast Jesse's role with an ex-wrestler. I was ordered to report to begin filming a week after Jesse's funeral. I didn't. They recast my role with a rapper – or "rhythmic linguist," as his publicist insisted he be called.

I beat myself up a lot for not having seen the warning signs about Jesse. Everything is clear in retrospect, now that I've read his diaries and know the feelings of failure and hopelessness he didn't want anyone to know.

He was a great actor, Jesse "not my real last name" Newman. The only person he wasn't good enough to fool was himself.

Sometimes I get so used to feeling sad that I forget the reason why I'm sad. I catch myself thinking that I should call Jesse so he can cheer me up. Then I remember why I'm sad.

I've always had this perplexing habit of staring at my own reflection when I'm depressed, getting lost in the mirror's image that tries so hard to be me but can never be more than two dimensions. Now, sometimes when I stare in the mirror I forget it's me all together. Sometimes I see Jesse.

Maybe I'm crazy. Maybe Jesse was the person I always wanted to be so I created him because I couldn't be him. Maybe Jesse was the person I didn't want to be, so I externalized him. Maybe I'm just not a strong enough person to live my life without my best friend so I waste my time staring in the mirror trying to convince myself he wasn't real because that way he's not really gone.

My agent won't even submit me for any real projects now. We both know I wouldn't be able to make it through a film shoot, not even a low budget film with even lower expectations. I don't even care enough to get up in the morning.

Steve's a good guy, though. He deserves better than dealing with Hollywood has-beens like me. He never will get to the next echelon of star clientele though. He cares too much, which is not an asset in the entertainment industry. It's not an asset in any business.

Steve knows I'm in no condition to do any real job. At the same time, he worries that if I don't work at all then I'll continue on a downward spiral past oblivion and straight into Neverland. So, he sets me up on no-brainer gigs. I do autograph signings and cameo appearances, things I can do drunk, drugged, and depressed and nobody cares even if they are the wiser.

Since the day I found Jesse I appeared as the Grand Marshal in the Thank Heaven Day parade in Christian Brothers, Missouri, where they put me up in a lovely Holiday Inn with complementary breakfast bar. I guest hosted a *Then Again* marathon on cable, complete with an authentic, outdated, K-Mart *Then Again* Halloween costume. And I sang the National Anthem at an Angels' game, without the benefit of either a breakfast bar or an outdated, plastic Halloween pullover.

I stopped returning Steve's calls when he asked if I'd play George Clooney in a Batman stunt show at a local theme park. They didn't want me to play Batman. They wanted me to play George Clooney as Batman. They didn't even want me specifically, but they'd be willing to use me.

That was about 9 months ago.

super freak

So, just what does one do after waking up in the washroom of a fast food restaurant in Hopewell, California? This afternoon I heard a train whistle in the distance. I thought about leaving my McDonald's perch and following the sound, finding the tracks and jumping a train. Not to get back home. What is home? LA? That's not a home, that's just where I live.

I wanted to jump the train to get away. Then I realized I already am away. That's the trouble with running away from something as opposed to running to something. When you're running to something, eventually you might get there. When all you're doing is running away from something, you never get where you're going because you don't know where you're going. You're going nowhere.

Of all the drugs I've done in my life, the one thing I never had any interest in was heroin. I've always thought of drugs as being something to add excitement to life, to accentuate it. Heroin is all about escape, it's about not caring. It's about not being. Heroin is the drug for those who want to run away. Suddenly it doesn't sound all that bad.

So what do I do now? Start walking back "home" to LA? Try to bum a ride from a stranger?

I guess I could try to call someone, try to get someone to come get me. Maybe my agent would if I promised to start working again, earn him some money. Then again, maybe after nine months of unreturned calls and years of bailing me out of jams, he's tired of my self-victimization routine.

I could start walking the other direction, see where the road leads. See if going somewhere else will make me whole again, if I ever was whole to begin with. I could see if LA is my problem, if being away from there will suddenly cure me of my evil ways.

Of course, if just not being in LA will make me a better person, I could just stay in Hopewell. Maybe get a job at the McDonalds. That might be setting my sights a bit high though. I mean obviously Mickey-D's is the pinnacle of success in this bustling road dent of a metropolis. But maybe I could start pumping gas at the Amoco station and eventually work my way up the ladder of success to a career with a paper hat, super sizing extra value meals.

I could do nothing at all. Make the decision to not make a decision. Take up a career as a statue, sitting in front of the famed Hopewell McDonalds. "Come One, Come All! See the amazing, nonmoving, nontalking fallen teen idol on display now in the McDonalds' parking lot, Hopewell's number one tourist attraction (the McDonalds, not the fallen idol)."

Growing up, I read a lot of comic books. One of my favorites was *Richie Rich*, the poor little rich boy. It's amazing I never played that role because I have the "poor me, pity me for having too much money and life handed to me on a plate" routine nailed down pat.

The fact is, I belong in LA – simply because I don't belong anywhere else. And I belong in show business – simply because I'm not qualified to do any real work.

Being a star isn't about being talented, it's not even about being lucky. Being a star is about simply not being qualified to be a real person. What we do on the screen or the television or the stage has no bearing on stardom. It's what the tabloids write about our fractured lives that makes us stars. You've got Julliard graduates living on food stamps because they can't get work as actors, but the guy who was in the headlines for having his pecker cut off by the wife he was abusing gets a three-picture deal – as soon as they get him a tutor to teach him how to spell his own name so he can sign the contract.

Maybe I'll check into a rehab clinic on the way back to LA. If it makes enough headlines, I'll get another movie deal.

Hats off to you, P.T. Barnum. You were right. All the public wants is to look at the freak show. The key to success isn't talent or drive or any of those self-help book theories. The key to success is being Rick James. You know – Super Freak.

about the author

After gaining fame as a child actor, Rikki Lee Travolta channeled his energies and creativity into earning his BA in Entertainment Management at the age of 15. Sporting a mixed lineage of Nez Perce and Italian bloodlines, as a leading man he has appeared nationally in headlining roles in Broadway musical classics and in concert as a best selling recording artist. Film, television, and stage credits include Shakespeare's *Hamlet* and *Romeo and Juliet*; Tennessee Williams' *A Streetcar Named Desire*, William Inge's *Picnic*; and Sir Andrew Lloyd Weber's *Joseph and the Amazing Technicolor Dreamcoat* and *Jesus Christ Superstar*; and work with Oscar winning director Ron Howard, Broadway legend Liza Minnelli, and Oscar nominated actor Woody Harrelson. He has guest starred in multiple theatrical companies of *Tony n' Tina's Wedding*, *West Side Story*, *Joseph*, *Bye Bye Birdie*, and *Guys and Dolls*. Rikki Lee studied at Chicago's famed *Second City* and is an internationally published magazine correspondent and playwright. Screenwriting credits include *Hero Before Dawn*, *Sacred Clone*, *Hangman*, and *Spirit Warrior*. Rikki Lee maintains addresses in Los Angeles and Chicago with his best friends Romeo and Gilligan and his one and only forever – Jessica Lauren. In between his performance schedule, he lends his efforts to charities and local civic organizations.

www.TravoltaNet.com